Twin Souls

Also by Lauren O. Thyme

Alternatives for Everyone, non-fiction
*Thymely Tales, Transformational Fairy Tales
for Adults and Children,* 2nd edition
Forgiveness Equals Fortune, non-fiction, co-written with Liah
Holtzman, 2nd edition
The Lemurian Way, Remembering your Essential Nature
Along the Nile, a novel on ancient Egypt
From the Depths of Thyme, a book of poetry
Strangers in Paradise, a novel of forgiveness
Cosmic Grandma Wisdom, non-fiction

Coming soon:
Catherine, A True Story

Twin Souls

A Karmic Love Story

Lauren O. Thyme

Lauren O. Thyme Publishing
Santa Fe
2017

First Edition

ISBN 978-0-9983446-1-4

Interior and Cover Design by Sue Stein
Cover photo by Kathy Fornal "Paris—Eros & Psyche photograph"
KathyFornal— FineArtAmerica.com
k.fornal@att.net 803-356-0183
Kathy Fornal.etsy.com

Lauren O. Thyme Publishing
Santa Fe, New Mexico
www.laurenothymecreations.com
thyme.lauren@gmail.com
Facebook Lauren O. Thyme

Thank you—
With love to Paul, without whom this story would never have been told.
To Mohamed the Magician, owner of Quest Tours,
who got me to places in Egypt I needed to see.
To Mohamed from Qena who took me to the crypt.

Contents

Preface

What are Twin Souls?

"The idea of twin souls is a spiritual, esoteric, or new age concept describing a special connection between two souls. Twin souls are thought to be a template or an archetype for an ancient/eternal type of relationship between lovers. According to mythology, in the beginning of time souls were split in half. Those souls would journey to Earth to learn and experience duality. Twin souls reincarnated over lifetimes with deep longing for the other half…until they finally reunited and left this physical plane as one. Twin souls assist in the ascension process for each other by aiding in the release of karma. When twin souls come together, they bring up any past emotions or experiences that need to be released. This can make being in a twin soul relationship difficult and painful, because often one person will lash out at the other and not truly understand why. This process is done because it prepares the twin souls to truly reunite and become one again when they ascend."—*Wikipedia*

"When twins come together, their chakras, kundalinis, and energy bodies experience great purging and cleansing that can be experienced as overwhelming, even excruciatingly painful. Often their connection to one another is so rigorous and overpowering that one or the other (or both) will run from the relationship."—-*Soulevolution.org*

Twin Souls:
- Before meeting each other, each twin experiences an unceasing, mysterious longing for a "special someone."
- The reunion of twin souls is rare.
- Twin souls, unlike soul mates, seldom incarnate together.
- The couple experiences love at first sight.
- They experience instant recognition at their first meeting along with a feeling of unfathomable oneness.
- They have a feeling of coming "home" when they meet.
- A raw, primal, intense passion, sexuality, and sensuality exists for and with each other. Unlike lust which diminishes with time, these feelings continue unabated and can even increase.
- The couple shares emotional, physical, and psychic pain when having to separate.
- An archetypal depth and breadth of romantic interaction exists, similar to that of Romeo and Juliet, Antony and Cleopatra, Zhivago and Lara, and Tristan and Isolde.
- The experience of deep, passionate, and romantic love is unlike anything ever experienced prior to meeting each other.
- They have trust and acceptance of each other from the beginning.
- Each is unable to hide feelings or thoughts from the other.
- They are affected by a feeling of inexplicable connection that never dies or diminishes.
- Telepathic communication of emotions, thoughts, feelings, and sexuality is common.

- Unbreakable bonds exist.
- When twin souls come together, the purpose is to heal themselves in the presence of the other.
- Often twins have a deep spiritual connection and sometimes have come together for a particular spiritual mission.
- Twin souls reunite near the end of their reincarnation cycle to finish: healing, learning, growing, evolving, and perhaps ascending.
- Generally a twin soul relationship is painful and difficult, because each person is a mirror for the other.
- Twin souls may experience many joyful reunions and painful separations.
- Twin souls have the ability to heal and soothe each other with their voices, even from a distance.
- Sometimes the experience of being together is so intense and difficult that it breaks the couple apart, but only physically. Yet their energy connection remains strong.
- Twin souls being together is exceedingly difficult and they may not be able to withstand a primary relationship.
- Twin souls have similar or completely opposite personalities, which exposes wounds in each twin in order to heal.

The bond between twin souls is so powerful that it can change each person's life, whether they are physically together or not, sometimes with enormous force and disruption of their former lives.

Often there are daunting hindrances to the twins being able to get together, such as being married to someone else, age differences, financial, geographical, health, or personality obstacles.

So if being with one's twin soul is so painful, challenging and problematic, what is the purpose of twin souls getting together?

As a soul is living his or her last lifetime, the call goes out to one's twin. This is to aid in concentrated healing of karma and wounds, leading to ascension. Ascension means finalizing one's journey through the earth plane of existence, ending a series of earth-bound lives, in order to move on together to the next dimension of learning and evolution.

Part One:

Twin Souls: A Karmic Love Story

Chapter One

THE DESERT WAS HOME TO SCORPIONS. Hawks. Crocodiles. Blistering heat in summer, yet cold in winter. Palm trees lined the banks of the undulating river, the Nile, a life-giving cradle to eight million souls in those days. Egypt, as we now call this country shrouded in enigma, was my birthplace.

My name was Kiya. I wasn't the daughter of nobility. I was a simple peasant girl. A precocious child. Strange and mystical. Born near the great temple of Dendera, the sacred holy place of Hathor.

Hathor had called to me in my youth. The great golden One whispered my name on the hot wind. Her silky voice was unmistakable. I could hear her deep inside me—a siren's call. I was smitten with adoration and vowed to offer my life to her in service. Even now, in the 21st century, I cannot see her beautiful face without feeling the familiar elation of recognition.

Back in those ancient days, even as a young child, I was receiving visions and hearing messages from beyond, and wanting to tell anyone within earshot about it. Without hesitation my parents sent me, their willful, hot-blooded, zealous child, to Dendera when I was nine. My father and mother could brag to neighbors that their child had been summoned by Hathor, an enormous honor.

My calling was worthy. Many young girls lived in the temple to assist and serve during the time of inundation, then returned to their families after the flood waters had subsided. To tend ducks and geese. Work in the family fields. Help raise their siblings. I, alone, from my village, would stay at Dendera throughout the year, for the rest of my life, to be taught the ancient mysteries of the Neter Hathor at Her Temple.

I was old enough to know the hymns to Hathor, yet young and innocent enough to believe those who served the Divine Ones in the various temples were untouchable, unaffected by human longings and frailties. I imagined those priests and priestesses as strong, devoted, and pure. I was thrilled to join their ranks.

During the first few years at Dendera I was given only mundane tasks: haul water from the sacred lake to cook, drink, and launder clothes. Unless the flood was low. If it was, I trekked all the way to the river, hauling the heavy goatskins dripping with the sacred water. I washed utensils and platters. Endlessly chopped onions. Plucked newly-killed ducks and geese for special joint feasts for the priestesses of Dendera and the priests of Kom-Ombo. Turned over the parched soil in our garden with wooden implements. Grew medicinal herbs and food.

Back-breaking work, but essential to the running of the Temple. Our work allowed those with more sacred tasks the time and energy to devote to Hathor. To heal people who arrived at Dendera in need of our services. To attend birthing mothers. Or to interpret dreams from visiting pilgrims who slumbered on our roof.

I was impatient as always. My desire to become a priestess was great, so I was barely able to keep myself in check much of the time. Sometimes my temper would flare and I would be banished from the Temple grounds, to stay in the visitor quarters outside the temple walls, until I was calm and tractable again. Yet in spite of all that, I was encouraged to stay, learn and serve.

Henite, a kind older Priestess recognized my talents while she forgave my bouts of emotion and encouraged others to forgive me as well.

One day she came to speak with me.

I put down the goatskin of water and waited for her.

Her thinning white hair floated around her head like clouds. The lines around her eyes were deeply creased in a perpetual smile. Flesh drooped from her chin while the sagging muscles on her skinny arms dangled and swung. But to me she was beautiful. My friend. My rescuer.

"Kiya, you must try to be more tolerant and wait for change to come. It always does." She smiled and touched my cheek gently. "You are still so very young. Just a child."

"Will you be my big sister?" I asked her impetuously.

"If you want me to be."

I vigorously shook my head yes.

"All right then. I agree to be your sister. If you promise me…"

"Yes, yes, I promise," I interrupted her.

Henite sighed good-naturedly and I returned to my chores.

She wanted to protect me from myself and to avoid punishments. I wasn't very obedient, but I kept trying. Meanwhile punishment was meted out to me regularly by a less-understanding Priestess, Weret-Imtes.

In my twelfth year, still considered an initiate, I progressed from mundane tasks and started taking lessons in the sacred mysteries.

First I learned about herbs and poultices, sacred for healing. For potent dreams. To reduce pain. To aid in childbirth. The Priestess in charge of these lessons was named Sitamun, renowned for her enthusiasm for eating. Thus her white linen gown hugged her plump body, threatening to break its threads.

I confess I wasn't interested in Sitamun's classes, which were too ordinary for me. I wanted to learn the fascinating and dramatic occult mysteries. As my child body changed into a woman during that year, and my hormones soared, visions and messages increased exponentially.

The next year I was trained with the sacred jewelry used during special rituals and rites, periodically getting them out for use, and then storing them away again in the crypt.

I loved climbing the ladder down to the narrow, dark passageway that curved to the stairs of the crypt, all the while holding a burning torch. Tiptoeing as though I was on a clandestine adventure. Then crawling through the small entryway, trying not to put out the torch, and stepping down a few steps to the dazzling, intricately carved limestone walls below. All this I accomplished in the care of Bunefer, an experienced Priestess in charge of the sacred jewelry.

Each item of jewelry was unpacked from storage with gentleness and reverence. Taking it out of its individual leather pouch, then unwinding the soft linen to reveal the treasured item within. I fondled each one, softly polishing it with the material from my short skirt until the metal and semi-precious gems gleamed. Then I would place the items in a tightly woven basket lined with soft animal hides, climb back to the Temple above with the precious items in my free hand.

When the ritual was complete, Bunefer and I would return the items and follow the procedure in reverse. I knew from gossip that many of the pieces of precious jewelry were ancient, having been in storage in the crypt long before anyone alive in Dendera temple could remember.

After a protracted time in training, and only if Bunefer was ailing, was I allowed to perform this procedure by myself. Sometimes I surreptitiously tried on an anklet or armlet or necklace, before taking them above ground, admiring the appearance and sensation of the devotional pieces on my body. Each item felt sensual and erotic, vibrating with energy. I sensed raw power surging through my body as I wore it.

One day Weret-Imtes followed me down to the crypt, since I was taking overly long in obtaining the sacred jewelry. She saw me standing in the crypt, my eyes closed in rapture, enjoying the effect of the jewelry I had donned.

"What do you think you are doing!? These are revered items!" Weret-Imtes admonished me. "Take them off immediately!" Her face red and her eyes glaring with anger, she pointed upstairs to my banishment. "Go to the visitors' quarters this moment!"

I was exiled once again. As I walked past other young girls and initiates on my departure, they chortled and giggled at my blushing humiliation; not the first time I had been in that situation. I gritted my teeth, feeling the muscles of my jaw tighten. I held my head high, as I pretended not to feel the sting of their critical and mocking words.

"I beg of you, Hathor," I prayed silently as I walked among them, stepping over the low mud-brick wall into the non-sacred area beyond, to endure my captivity once again. "Help me to learn to become a good priestess in your name." But I only felt the heat of humiliation rising from my bare neck up to my cheeks, with no response from the Divine One.

Some days after I returned to the Temple proper from my exile, Weret-Imtes permanently removed me from the task of jewelry caretaking. I was dismissed to the tiny room I shared with four other initiates to await new orders.

Henite, the officiating sunu hemet ntr Priestess and my protector, came to see me, as I sat slumped forlornly on the hard floor.

"Kiya, come to my chamber for a private chat."

Dutifully I got up and followed her, wondering if she would now finally abandon me, as others had done. My unforgiveable behavior turned them all away eventually. But her words surprised me.

"Kiya, I personally will oversee your lessons from this moment on. Do not divulge what we will be doing," she told me quietly, in a conspiratorial tone.

I was overwhelmed but glad for her continuing friendship.

Henite continued. "I have watched you for yearly inundations of Mother Nile. You have qualities and attributes most of the initiates do not have, and will never have. These qualities must be inborn. I have talked with a few people from your village who observed you from infancy, who confirmed my thoughts." She stared unblinking into my widening eyes, looking for confirmation.

I breathed deeply, hardly able to contain my excitement and relief. "I know what you are talking about, August Mistress. I cannot seem to fit in with the others. I argue and get into trouble. They are always scorning me. But they cannot hear, see, and sense what I can."

The older hemet ntr Priestess touched my shoulder affectionately with her fingertips. "Your gifts are at once a blessing as well as a curse. I hope that together we can assist your gifts to evolve into something helpful to others. You have been born near this temple, given messages, and sent here to study for reasons that are mostly beyond my reckoning. Together we will learn what those reasons are." Then Henite hugged me.

All my despair and loneliness evaporated in that moment as I felt her thin arms embrace me in acceptance.

She then held me at arm's length. "You have multiple talents, Kiya. I will attempt to move you in many directions at once, to deepen and grow." She smiled.

"Thank you, my dearest Priestess Sister. I hope I honor you in my education."

"Much of what I will teach you is hallowed beyond most Priestess' understanding. Kiya, you must be extremely careful not to impart to anyone else here at Dendera what I alone will explain and demonstrate to you and what you will experience from it. You will move permanently into my private chamber here for tutoring."

I nodded in agreement.

Henite continued. "I was taught by a very holy woman who lived here many inundations ago, who is long dead and now resides with

Osiris in the afterlife. She told me what I am telling you. She taught me mysteries within mysteries. I had hoped to find the right young woman I could share this extraordinary knowledge with before I, too, depart for the Duat. You are that girl, Kiya."

"I am?" I was shocked, yet pleased.

"Yes, my dear. You are to be the recipient of my expertise. When I am gone, you too will find a girl to teach these things to, to pass on this holy lineage. You will know that girl when she arrives, although it might take numerous inundations before she arrives. Do you agree to do so?"

"I...I think so," I stuttered. I didn't actually know what she was referring to nor what I was agreeing with.

I studied with Henite, my Priestess mentor, every day often until late at night by the glow of a flickering oil lamp. The other Priestesses were glad to be rid of me, along with my emotional outbursts, over-confident manner, and annoying behavior. Most especially relieved was the senior web hemet ntr Priestess Weret-Imtes, the Priestess I had in-furiated by wearing the sacred jewelry, among many other offenses. I was glad to escape her glaring looks and downturned lips.

Henite trained me in everything she had ever been taught, learned, intuited, and observed in her many years at the Temple of Hathor at Dendera. She was wise, patient, kind, and eager to impart her knowl-edge to me. In turn I adored her as a mother, sister, friend, and col-league, quickly absorbing all that she passed on.

My initial lessons were that of extrasensory reinforcement—learning to receive verbal, visual, and sensate messages from Hathor and other Neterw. I already had native talent in these areas. Henite helped me strengthen them. Then to trust the messages and apply them as appropri-ate. I learned how to clearly articulate what I was receiving. Since I already innately possessed paranormal abilities, my learning advanced quickly.

Next Henite taught me the laying on of hands for healing, relief of pain, and for calming troubled souls, increasing the energy by asking for assistance from Hathor. When I had learned enough to my teacher's satisfaction, she and I took patients into a private sanctuary, where I practiced unobserved by others of the Temple. I amazed myself at how much healing I was able to transmit. This was a gift I didn't know I possessed.

When I turned fourteen, my sister hemet ntr Priestess took me into our chamber for a private conversation. Henite sat down in a cross-legged chair and motioned for me to sit on the ground near her. She hesitated, looking for the appropriate words. She appeared very solemn. I waited attentively. Finally she spoke. "Kiya, you have become a woman in the last two years. Your body, spirit, emotions, and sensations have matured as well."

I blushed, looking down, noticing my long, slender arms and legs, flat belly and soft, gently curved breasts.

"You have a dancer's body," my mentor Priestess continued. "Similar to some temple images you see carved on the Temple walls here at Dendera. You have an appearance that functions in harmony with your talents. Your looks are often the standard for the task at hand."

"I don't understand, Sister." I had grown to call her that familiar word and Henite accepted it without question.

"I am going to teach you things that can only be taught by someone who is very skilled and well-trained. This ability emanates from the holy of holies, from Hathor herself. A sunu hemet ntr Priestess of this distinction must be intuitive, healing, and compassionate. Even more importantly is that she is in touch with her emotions, sensuality, and sexuality. All those abilities you possess."

"What am I supposed to do with these?" I interrupted.

My Sister Priestess shook her head gently at my outburst and continued. "Healing and sensual energies will be drawn into your physical body, then directed to the person you are working with." She corrected herself. "The man you are working with."

"A man? What man?"

Henite paused and went on. "That man might be a nobleman. Or a Priest. He could even be Pharaoh." She paused to let the information sink in.

"I can't do that, Sister! That task is for a wife, not for me. I'm learning to be a priestess, not a spouse! I have surrendered my life to this holy temple, to learn sacred mysteries. What are you telling me?" I began to cry in fear and disgust.

"Kiya," Henite said my name soothingly, but it didn't help.

"I am not going to be with a Priest. Not with Pharaoh. I am not a prostitute!" I exclaimed in indignation. Yet at the same time I could feel my female parts vibrate and be stimulated with an energy I had never felt so strongly before.

"No, Kiya, of course you are not a prostitute. I am talking about the greatly honed skill of a sacred healing Priestess. This ability is to help heal, revive, and refresh a man who is in need of your assistance. Not an ordinary man. A man who is also dedicated to the well-being of our country. Who is, like you, in the service of the Neterw. Something an ordinary wife cannot do, is not trained to do. Sometimes powerful men are in need of this consecrated assistance and only a sacred healing Priestess can help."

I wrinkled my forehead in confusion, about to speak.

Henite put her hand up and looked at me with loving but firm understanding and kindness. "Fear not. You will not be, are not, a prostitute. Although a woman of the night has her special place in this world as well as any other. But that is another matter." She waved any questions away. "You will become an extraordinary Priestess, with talents you will possess and wield with love, grace, sensuality, and sacredness. Hathor herself will guide you and you will become the embodiment of the Neter of physical love."

I put my head on Henite's knee and wept. "No, I cannot. I cannot do this. I cannot learn this. This is too much for me."

Sister stroked my wet face and crooned her words. "This is a job Hathor chose you to occupy. You cannot refuse. You are to become Hathor's holy vessel. It is what you were born to do, led here to Dendera and your destiny. Step by step. Year by year."

I shivered in fear, but also with a growing curiosity. My tears stopped. "But can I do it?"

"Of course, Kiya. You are a perfect embodiment, otherwise I would not be here talking to you, teaching you. I will help you to learn much of the details and techniques involved. However, the inner education, the wisdom you will bring into your body, only Hathor Herself can teach you."

I sat up and wiped my face, my interest growing with every passing second. "Did Hathor teach you too?"

"Yes, She did." Henite smiled with a knowing smile. "Hathor is the most profound of all teachers. Wise. Kind. Ferociously, intensely sexual and physical. Yet also deeply loving and gentle. Just as you will become under our—Hathor's and my—tutelage."

"How can I heal someone like that? A man, I mean."

"Mistress Hathor will be with you during every healing encounter. She will take over your khat and your khu. You will enter a dream-like state when Hathor joins with you, yet you will remember everything that takes place. Pleasure for both you and the man will be deeply felt, intense, ecstatic, blissful, as if you are flying through the Duat on Nuit's body, experiencing every pleasure and delight that a body can feel. Free of all concerns and worries. Leaving behind all pain and discomfort." Henite closed her eyes as she explained. I knew she had experienced firsthand what she was describing.

"And since Hathor is the spiritual mother of our beloved land, Her pampering will fill the man as well, through you. He will feel content, nurtured by the encounter, as if he is a suckling babe in arms. This coming together of you, the Neter, and the man is an experience no one can create without Hathor's intervention, without proper, long-term training, and without natural proclivities such as you have. It is an extraordinary gift. You have that gift and are being called to present this gift soon."

"Soon?" Suddenly I was afraid again. I shivered in apprehension.

"Yes. Soon. But not before you are ready. Oh, and one more thing. The man that you will connect with will have had some of his own training and natural skills as well. The two of you will unite as effortlessly, as closely, as twins in a womb. Like Isis and Osiris."

"Umm." I felt drowsy already, as if I was already undergoing the blissful coupling yet to come. Soon. "I'm ready, my Sister."

"Yes, you are." Henite leaned over and kissed me sweetly on my forehead. "The man will be carefully selected in advance. Nothing will be left to chance nor personal interest, nor attraction, nor lust. This is not a love meeting as such, but a consecrated one. The coupling must be correct, at the proper time and place. The sacred meeting is selected in advance by those in authority."

"I understand," I agreed. But I really didn't understand, nor would I for a long time to come.

Chapter Two

ALTHOUGH MY TRAINING INTENSIFIED, I was still considered an initiate. I wasn't sure when my status would ultimately change from initiate to Priestess. But I was satisfied to prepare myself for what lay ahead.

Special clothing was selected for me to wear for the all-important occasions of sacred healing contact, not for everyday use. Dresses, skirts, and shawls of the best linen possible, with fine threads that made the fabric smooth and silky, were sewn for me. My head was shaved regularly. I was given two wigs to choose from, each made from healthy, luminous human hair. I wore the more modest wig every day; the other was meant for the extraordinary healing rites to come.

Special pieces of jewelry were cast exclusively for me to adorn myself. I was given an armlet made of malachite. Two anklets of turquoise with tinkling copper bells to jingle wherever I walked. A necklace fashioned with connected beads of lapis lazuli with a golden Hathor pendant attached. I was also given a circular gold ring pounded thinly to wear on my index finger. But my favorite item was a silver cuff with a huge piece of amber attached to it.

No longer did I have to sneak into the crypt to try on jewelry, hiding from the watchful eye of the senior web hemet ntr Priestess, Weret-Imtes. These items were mine to decorate myself as I pleased and belonged only to me. However, I wore this jewelry only in private during my training. These were meant for my eyes only. And my teacher Henite. And ultimately a special man.

I was also taught how to apply make-up, primarily green eye paint from powdered malachite, and kohl to outline my eyes. Cosmetics had a magical quality imbued in them as well as to accentuate attractiveness. I applied makeup during practice session, not in the Temple.

No longer would I go barefoot, as the bottom of my feet became calloused by sand and sharp stones. Sandals made from pliable kid goat leather were provided for me for everyday use.

I rubbed my feet, indeed all of my body, with oils to make the skin soft and luxuriant. I was encouraged to apply fragrant khyphi and sandalwood during practice times, which made me dizzy from the potent smells.

Before all these personal items were given to me, they were blessed in ritual by Dendera priestesses in sacred ceremonies using myrrh, frankincense, sistrums, dancing, and chanting. The holy energy from all the items thus ritualized added to the abilities I already possessed. Hathor was the Neter of beauty. So I, as her Priestess, would bestow beauty and femininity through socially-defined, cultural attributes such as clothing, jewelry, and make-up, as well as my natural womanly assets and sensitivities, and the magical energy I would channel.

I wasn't a beautiful woman, but wearing these items enhanced my personal vitality to both appear as if, and to feel as though, I was beautiful.

Naturally I needed to be adorned properly to be deemed worthy enough to be intimate in sacred healing union with a High Priest, Vizier, or even Pharaoh. With all the attention being shown to me, I felt as though I had become a royal woman of distinction. But in reality I was still an initiate, a young girl preparing in earnest for one of the most rigorous, unusual vocations a priestess could attain. Not only did the smells of kyphi and sandalwood go to my head, but unfortunately my sense of self-importance did too. That would soon come to an end as I diligently trained.

I was given a small room adjacent to that of my Sister Priestess, so that we could continue my intensified training at all hours of the day or night. Also, so she could keep a watchful eye on me.

All my precious new items were kept in a woven basket in my chamber. Exotic scents of sandalwood and kyphi emanated from the tiny holes of the hamper, pervaded the enclosure with their perfume, and lent a heady aroma to all my belongings. I had a simple straw mattress with a soft covering to lay upon, not as much as I deemed myself worthy of, but for once I didn't complain. Eventually, when I had an encounter with a powerful man, we would meet in a more elevated place than my humble bedchamber, in accomodations which would be sanctified for the holy encounter.

Every day I practiced with my Sister Priestess. In the privacy of my room, she ignited a small cube of myrrh in an alabaster dish, the favorite fragrance of Hathor. Then I washed myself from head to foot, dressed in a fine gown from the basket, pulled on sandals, donned the best wig, makeup my eyes, dabbed kyphi or sandalwood on myself, and then fastened my jewelry to finger, arms, ankles, and neck. With each step of the process, as I dressed and adorned myself, I could feel the vitality grow. Vibrating through my private parts and backside. Rising up my body, flowing upwards through my chest and breasts, throat, forehead. Then emerging out the top of my head in a shower of sparkling light. By the time I finished dressing, I felt like a different person. Elegant. Holy. Sensuous. Beautiful. Desirable. These physical items magically transmuted me into the Golden Neter Hathor. I can't explain how wearing these could make such a difference to my body and senses; all I know is that they did.

I was trained to stand in my tiny chamber with no company except my Sister, feeling every nuance of tingling and sensation in my body. After standing for hours each day, ready to collapse with exhaustion, I at last removed all items of clothing, sandals, and jewelry. Stored them away in the basket. Washed clean my face and dressed in my simple short initiate's skirt once again, breasts bare. Every day I could feel a little more power emanating throughout my body.

Sister told me that eating would reduce the sensations I experienced. So only after I finished with my daily exercise was I allowed to eat. Ravenously I ate the bread and beer of the day's meal and rested. Sometimes I was allowed dried grapes or a piece of salted fish. Late in the day I joined the other girls, initiates, and Priestesses at the evening meal.

I was admonished to speak to no one at supper. With great effort I finally achieved that ability, often forgetting and initiating conversations.

My Sister Priestess would then clear her throat, the signal that I was disobeying. Whenever I heard her subtle cue, I stopped talking at once. In time I remained mute as the stones of the Temple, focusing my attention inward during every evening meal.

After thirty or more days of dressing-up exercises, I vibrated and shook with the power of the potency that arose within me. I had learned to stand in place, transfixed, calm, and silent unless told otherwise.

My second tier of lessons with my Sister Priestess, amazingly enough after practicing silence, were word games. Not ordinary words, but those having to do with every part of the physical anatomy, both male and female. I practiced with two life-size drawings on papyrus, one of a man and the other a woman. I was taught to point to a spot, then use the sacred word to name it, avoiding all mention of slang. The common jargon, I was told, insulted Hathor. Therefore, I learned only the appropriate, official word for each feature.

I concentrated initially on the nude female body, until I was able to name each part with its appropriate word without mistake. Then I followed suit with the portrait of a naked man, blushing at the features I was not personally acquainted with, but soon learned. Thus I was able to observe, name out loud, and touch with my fingertip each place of human anatomy, serenely, without laughing or embarrassment, until each sacred word and contact became effortless and second-nature.

The next phase to practice and memorize were litanies relating to Hathor of various lengths, praising Her and invoking Her presence.

A Priestess in the Temple had learned these as well and spoke them during rituals and rites. However, for me, speaking these invocations was meant to be highly personal, as I was Hathor's stand-in during a particular sacred healing ritual. Only the man and I would hear my invocations, whispered softly, rather than loudly enough for an entire Temple congregation to overhear.

The fourth phase in my preparation was to incorporate all of the previous steps. Dressing. Standing. Feeling the energy course through me in silence. Touching and speaking to a human form. Invoking Hathor. Willful and stubborn as I was, I applied those strengths to learning. Within a comparatively short time, according to my Sister, I was able to combine all the steps smoothly and gracefully.

"You have done well. Let us take a few days to relax and celebrate." She smiled and hugged me to her.

I was more than happy to comply. She had been relentless in my schooling and I could use some rest. However, my respite was cut short.

The next day my sister visited me in my small chamber. I had been playing with my amber bracelet when she arrived. "I have been informed that you are to face the first test in your new role."

"What!? Why?" I was perplexed and suddenly irritated. "I'm not ready yet, am I?"

"Those in authority believe you are ready." She grimaced. "My dearest, I am not allowed, nor are you, to question these decisions. Have I not taught you obedience and silence?"

"Yes, but..."

She cleared her throat and gave me a look to silence all my demands. "No. We will speak no further of this." Her word was final.

"May I ask when?" I tried to summon up humility I didn't feel.

"Tomorrow," was her curt reply.

"Tomorrow?! That's too soon. Who is it to be?" I persisted. "Who is he?"

"It does not matter. I can tell you he is a man of high rank."

I exhaled loudly.

"You must promise me to do all I have taught you. In good humor," she added.

I pursed my lips and pouted.

Henite ignored my protests. "Go rest now. And take your supper... . in silence." She moved quickly to her chamber, leaving me behind.

I didn't know that Henite was as angry as me. My education had been cut critically short, over her many protestations. The wheel of karma was beginning to turn and no one could stop its spinning out of control.

Chapter Three

THE NEXT DAY I WAITED. Dressed. Bejeweled. Perfumed. Sandaled. Coifed. With eyes made-up. I stood in the narrow corridor outside my bed chamber, waiting. Rivulets of sweat dripped down my face. I had learned to stand in serene silence. However, internally I was quaking with trepidation.

Around midday Sister finally approached with an imposing man at her side. I had never before seen a man in the private Priestess quarters of Dendera Temple. He was tall, dressed in simple garb, rather than that of a man of power.

"This is Seneb, High Priest of Sobek…" Sister began her formal introduction but she was cut short.

"One moment." The man studied me, appraising me as if I was a lamb for sale in the market. Quickly he evaluated my body, features, face, as well as my ceremonial garb. His mouth turned upwards in an approving smile. He turned to Henite and spoke. "Leave us," he told her curtly.

"But Kiya is not yet fully trained," Sister retorted quickly, hoping to dissuade him.

"No matter," was his reply. "Leave."

Her face turned pale and she left. I could hear her straw sandals making flip-flopping noises on the stone floor, as she disappeared from view.

The High Priest appeared to be more than thirty inundations old, although I'm not a good judge of someone's age. He wore a simple nemes rather than the elaborate headdress of a High Priest. His floor-length unadorned robe was whitest linen, not fine like my own, but stiffer fabric.

The robe had short sleeves, so I could see he had strong, muscular arms. Taller than me, the hard pectoral muscles of his broad, hairless chest were carved in a robust masculinity different from my own soft breasts. His freshly shaved head gleamed.

Some would call him handsome, with the bony structure of his cheeks high in elegant relief. But his hawk-like nose altered his features and gave him a commanding, imperious appearance. His thick sensuous lips were curved upwards in a perpetual smile, the lines around his mouth etched deep.

He had solid hands with a stout thumb and long, tapering fingers, indicative of someone who was exceedingly psychic and intuitive, and a healer as well.

I studied him but his face was impenetrable, though I excelled at reading people's countenances.

His eyes were unlike any I had ever seen. They were the color of succulent papyrus reeds. The eyelids slanted at the edges, giving him a mysterious appearance. The arching bony structure where eyebrows would have been was freshly plucked.

Then he narrowed his eyes, tilted his head, and looked at me from the side of his eyes, reptilian like.

I sucked in my breath, suddenly on fire.

Although I had endlessly practiced wearing the sacred outfit of Hathor and feeling the immense energy rush throughout my body, nothing had prepared me for the surge of craving I felt for Seneb. As though without a word I had become his willing, adoring slave. Wanting to touch him and be touched by him.

Unable to take my eyes away from his sensual, unblinking gaze, his look made me feel helpless in his presence, unable to do anything except what he wished me to do, not even able to move a single muscle.

I remembered every nook and cranny of the masculine body I had studied in my classes. But his body was different from the lifeless drawing I had scrutinized so intently. Seneb was vitally alive with masculine energy and prowess. Under his robe protruded a huge hard lump below his waist cord. Not the helpless piece of flesh I had devoted to memorizing, but a demanding presence of maleness that made me want to move my body against it.

I could feel a pull, an unwitting attraction towards him. I wanted to become Hathor for him. With him. No. To be fully, deliciously myself. As I had never known myself before now.

Observing my bewilderment, then the awakening of interest, he laughed. A humorous, melodious, deep baritone laugh. A laugh filled with the joy of living fully. Sensually. Supremely confident in his own masculinity. This High Priest of Sobek gave deference to no other living person except perhaps Pharaoh. Seneb was his own man. Subservient to no one. Certainly not to an initiate like me. I was nothing. Less than nothing. Not yet even a Priestess, yet more than a girl. Although I was fully decorated in the elaborate paraphernalia of a sacred sunu hemet ntr Hathor Priestess, a sexual healing Priestess, I was his to command.

"Come here," he murmured, slyly smiling at me.

I stepped like one in a trance, moving closer to him and looked up into his face, shaded by a Hathor column behind him.

Without another word, he wrapped his strong arms around my waist, and pulled me to him, then kissed me. Opening my mouth with his tongue, I could feel his strong white teeth under full lips. His tongue explored mine, sucking, before plunging itself into my mouth.

Having never kissed a man, never mind a High Priest, I was stunned. But only for a split second. I returned his kiss joyfully.

This encounter was nothing that I had been trained for nor prepared for. Seneb was nothing I was ready for. Days and weeks of practicing energy coming into and up my body in waves of sacred ecstasy was now mirrored in male flesh. I was defenseless over myself. Powerless to resist. Unable to do anything except kiss him back, touching my tongue to his, moving my body up against him.

Feeling the bulge—and his excitement and raw manly power—seducing me. Overtaking me. Capturing me with his desire. Like the cobra neter rising up. Merging with me, and becoming one. I felt dizzy.

Then he broke from our embrace. He firmly took hold of my hand and drew me into my tiny chamber. I could hardly breathe. Couldn't think. What had I been taught to do? All my training disappeared in that moment.

As we entered my chamber, I huskily whispered words I half remembered. "Hathor, bless this man and our sacred union."

My words seemed to inflame his desire. He yanked my gown up over my head and threw it to the ground. I stood naked except for my jewelry. He pulled off his nemes and his own robe, then positioned us to sit on my straw mattress. He removed our sandals.

He helped me to lay down, and he lay next to me, stroking my breasts, moving his body so that his knee was firmly positioned between my legs, pressing against my feminine mound, then kissed me deeply again. My labia pulsated with excitement. My nipples erected high and firm.

"Wait!" I wanted to protest. "This isn't proper. We're supposed to lie somewhere else. Do something else." No words came out. Only an instinctive groan of desire emerged from inside me.

My arduous training to become a Priestess of Hathor vanished. All I wanted was Seneb. Only Seneb. Forever. For him never to leave my side. Never to stop his excitement. Or mine. To be one with him, in the space of my room. Nothing mattered anymore. To be with him, touching, kissing, stroking. His skin against my skin, merging as one.

"Touch me down here," I implored.

And so he did. Touched me with his long searching fingers. After a bit he maneuvered me with his legs to lie flat, then slithered on top of me. Spreading my legs wide, he plunged his hard mass into me. I felt a sharp, quick pain, then waves of pleasure.

For hours. Or was it days? Lifetimes? He didn't stop. I didn't want him to stop.

Was this Hathor I was experiencing? Or myself? I felt desire so all-encompassing it bypassed my mind. My body was having a life of its own beyond mere thoughts. Moving on its own. Desiring on its own.

At one point I thought I heard voices echoing outside my chamber, discussing. Or was it arguing? But the voices soon disappeared and all was silence. Except our mutual heavy breathing. Dampness of our bodies in heat together. My cries of rapture as he moved slowly inside me, then rapidly, then slowly again. Stopping his thrusting at times, then beginning again.

I arched my back to meet him, to feel him deep inside me, wrapping my long legs tightly around his waist, to be in tune with his movements.

As my chamber darkened with the progression of the sun outside, he moved inside me very rapidly, then stopped. "Kiya!" He rasped in orgasm. His body shuddered and quivered.

The sound of my name from his lips dove deep into my chest, like a bird flying free.

Spent, he lay on top of me, his breathing slowing. His body relaxing. I put my arms around him and held his sweaty body close, willing him to stay inside me. My legs still entwined around him. Never to let him go. "Don't stop," I begged him. He looked at me and smiled carelessly, like Bastet the cat Neter. The smiling lines around his mouth inexplicably thrilled me. I hoped he would never stop smiling at me that way. Loving me that way.

"Never stop," I whispered as our joining begin to shrivel. Not a demand. Merely a supplication from an initiate to the High Priest of Kom-Ombo.

He rolled off me. Then enfolded me in his arms and we slept.

Chapter Four

I MUST HAVE SLUMBERED a long time in that drowsy late afternoon bliss following lovemaking. When I awoke Seneb was gone.

I sat up, suddenly chilled, an ache in my chest. I looked around my chamber. My gown was there but his nemes, robe, and sandals were missing.

I felt stickiness between my legs and looked down. Seneb's semen was mixed with my virginal blood, smeared across my thighs and groin.

I got up shakily. First I took off all my jewelry and carefully placed the precious pieces in the basket. I went to the vessel of water in the corner and washed myself thoroughly. Then put on my initiate's short skirt, although I was still damp.

As I went to the entry of my room and peered out guiltily, I saw no one. The sun must have set since the Temple was darkening.

Shame, as strong as my earlier desire, flooded me. I was vitally aware of all that had transpired between the High Priest and me. I knew, without Sister telling me, that I had not performed the task I was trained to do. I had failed in my mission. All the long years of preparation were dust. I was now a dirty thing, a rag to be disposed of. Unclean. Failed as a Priestess. Undesirable as a woman.

Bitter tears dripped down my cheeks. My throat burned with the recognition of my ignominy. I was worse than any nasty jackal that roamed the desert, eating rotting flesh.

Suddenly my body reminded me of the ecstasy I had lived through with Seneb that fateful afternoon. My sexual desire rose like an untended weed in the Temple garden.

But…He. Was. Gone.

The word "gone" had an ominous sound to it. Like the end of life.

I remembered dying patients who had been treated in the Temple. How they looked when their Ba had departed their Khat. One moment…life. The next…absence of life. An empty shell. A husk of flesh. Although I had seen dead bodies many times, I never got used to the finality of death and the absence of any animating flesh. Mouths hung slackly open. Eyes rolled back, unseeing. Pupils enlarging until they filled entire eyes like black stones. Bodies cooling. Stiffening. The Ba never came back.

Would Seneb come back to me? He was a High Priest and I, an initiate. No. No longer an initiate. I wasn't sure what I was nor what the future held for me now. "Oh, Hathor!" I shrieked, the sound coming from my soul. Two words of anguish echoing in the empty passageway.

Instantly, Henite my Sister Priestess was at my side. She had been waiting in her own chamber, motionless as a recently-engorged snake, to come to me. She put her arms tenderly around me while I blubbered my regrets. My failures. My illicit love.

"What shall I do?" I asked. "Where shall I go? I can't go back to my village. My parents will be mortified."

"You will continue to live here of course," Henite comforted me. "You have done no wrong."

"I haven't?"

"No. Nothing that happened was your fault. He knew better. Seneb is a powerful man. He took advantage of you. He is used to getting his way." I saw her cheekbones rise as she clenched her teeth.

"What now?" I asked meekly, unable to take in all that she told me.

"I don't know, Kiya." She shrugged desolately.

"Will he be back?"

"No…" She shook her head slowly. "I don't think so."

My spirits sunk low. I moved away from her toward my mattress and collapsed upon it. It silently reminded me of what had transpired. How my life had unalterably changed that afternoon. First rising in passion. In union with my beloved. Then falling into absolute despair.

Henite sat down next to me, wordless now, holding my hand.

I couldn't feel the pressure of her affection. I was numb and empty, the future bleak as the vast desert around us.

For days afterwards I mourned uncontrollably. I ate little. I had no appetite. Guilt and shame and grief were my companions, faithful in their solemn duty towards me. Whenever I wandered around the Temple, all those I met avoided my glance, looking down at their feet or off into the distance. I knew from their pitying or judgmental looks that everyone had heard of my misdeed. I avoided the entire female society of the Temple and stayed in my chamber. Only Sister visited me, bringing me food, and friendship.

All my new, valuable possessions were taken from me, except for the clothing, a pair of sandal,s and the amber bracelet. I felt like an accidental thief, who had stolen things that didn't belong to me without knowing or understanding. And now Temple law judged I be punished for the robbery by taking my precious items away from me.

One night when the moon was waxing full, I took a walk, relieved to be outside, far away from judgmental eyes. I wandered past the columns, near the mud brick enclosure. The hour was very late. All was silent. The girls, initiates, and Priestesses of the Temple were asleep.

Distant stars of the Duat blinked at me from the black sky above, unconcerned with my troubles.

I then heard a voice in my head, calling me. Or was it floating on the wind? It was a familiar, masculine voice. His voice. Seneb.

"Hello," the voice said casually, as if it was the most natural thing in the world to be talking to me.

Was I imagining it? Could it be him? "Hello, yourself," I said, testing my sanity.

"I have missed you, Kiya." The words teased me.

"Is it you?" I asked.

"Of course, my darling. Who else would it be?"

I looked around but saw no one. "This can't be happening," I thought to myself.

Seneb's voice replied. "Why not? In all your studying, surely you have experienced a mind link at times."

Startled that the voice could hear my innermost thoughts, I said, "Yes, but not on purpose."

"What purpose?" the voice queried.

"Stop it!" I was suddenly angry at the disembodied voice. "You're bothering me."

"But you like to be bothered, don't you, Kiya?" the voice seductively played with me. "In fact, I remember how much you like to be bothered. It makes you wet."

"That's enough, Seneb!" I exclaimed. "You've dishonored me once. I won't allow you to do it again!" How bizarre to be having a conversation with a khabit, a ghostly presence.

"I couldn't help myself," the voice continued. "You played a role in this as much as me."

Did I detect a note of sadness?

Seneb continued. "I heard that you were being trained, were in training, to become the next sunu healing Priestess who would embody

Hathor. In my lifetime there has only been one, and she was much older than me. Not to my liking."

"Sister?"

"Is that what you call her?"

"Yes, Henite is my spiritual sister."

"Hm. Interesting." Seneb continued his tale. "When I searched through Dendera, I found you quickly. You were unmistakable, unlike any other woman at the Temple. I watched you as you developed. Followed you mentally as you passed one test after another. For almost an inundation I got to know you intimately."

"You never met me," I replied.

"No, not in my physical body. But I can travel without it, moving about in my Ba. I've been highly trained in many abilities. Plus I have natural proclivities, just as you do. Did you not ever see me? Sense me?"

Maybe I did, but I lied. "Not once."

"Well, that's a shame. I could feel and see you easily. I grew fond of you. I watched you grow in wisdom, taking on the persona of Hathor. But I couldn't wait any longer. I had to be with you. Touch you. Make love with you."

"Couldn't wait? But shouldn't you have asked about me? Asked if I wanted to be with you?"

"No. There was only a limited opportunity for us to meet. You were being prepared for someone else."

"Who?"

"That's not important. I wanted, needed, to be your first. The most important man in your life."

"Why?"

"Because we are attached."

"But I wasn't ready for you yet," I accused him.

"I was told that."

"But that didn't matter to you? I don't matter to you?" I replied hotly.

"You matter a great deal. Kiya, you may never understand. I...I may never understand," the voice murmured. "While I became acquainted with you, I discovered an immense connection. Between you and me. We are one soul, Kiya. This coupling between souls only happens rarely."

"Yes," I slowly answered, after digesting his words. I remembered our lovemaking, the power we had together. "An immense connection indeed." I listened but no more was forthcoming. I waited, then impulsively asked, "So what now?"

"Now?" An intake of breath. "I don't know." A clearing of a throat. Then Seneb's masculine voice. "Forget about me. Go on with your life without me."

"I can't do that," I replied with sadness and certainty.

"Too bad." The voice took on a hopeful tone. "But I have an idea that may help both of us."

"Tell me."

"Return to your bedchamber."

"What?"

"I will join you there."

"I'm confused...You're at Kom-Ombo, aren't you?"

"Yes."

"But then...?"

"Kiya, go to your bedchamber and wait for me there."

"All right." I hurried through the dark night and the silent corridors, back to my tiny room.

Seneb continued to instruct me. "Take off your clothes and lay down."

I did as I was told. Breathlessly, in my quiet room, I waited for what was next. I could never have imagined what he was capable of. Suddenly his Ba was lying on the mattress next to me. Unmistakably him. His energy. His masculine authority. I felt the same tremendous surge of excitement as I had that day when we met. I could even feel his physical presence. He was with me.

"Kiya, tell no one I have come here," he said. "Promise me."

"I promise, Seneb."

For that agreement, he kissed me, devouring me with his lips and his mouth.

I could feel his knee's pressure to my groin and I cried out. "Seneb!" I closed my eyes and thrilled to the sensations of him. I felt everything he did with me as though he was there in a body. We made love in every conceivable way, in every imaginable position, our bodies hungry for each other, until just before dawn. After his Ba departed, I fell asleep, smiling to myself, satisfied, yet greedy for more.

Very late the following night I waited anxiously for him on my mattress, naked, hoping he would appear. He didn't disappoint me. The first thing I felt was his kiss. Then his knee.

Night after delirious night, Seneb arrived after the Temple was asleep and we made love until dawn. I hoped the Priests of Kom-Ombo were sleeping as well, so no one in either Temple would be disturbed. That no one would guess our secret.

Sister noticed the change in me. "You have healed your sadness?" Henite inquired.

"Yes," and blushed.

"I have inquired about you continuing to live here," Henite changed the subject.

"Oh?" I looked at my feet, not daring to meet her gaze, for fear she would intuit my guilty secret.

"You will be allowed to stay here the rest of your natural life. However, your former studies will be discontinued. Nor will you be allowed to go through any other Priestess training that is offered here. Your status will be changed from initiate to Temple Seer. You will be allowed, after much persuasion from me, to be able to use your talents to help us at Dendera."

"Thank you!" I exclaimed, now doubly excited.

"You will be closely observed, however, to make sure that the sanctity of this Temple remains inviolate."

I gulped, remembering the secret with the High Priest and my promise. "Yes, Sister, I understand." I hated lying to her, but I had no other choice.

My Sister Priestess smiled wearily. "I am very tired after the last few days. I deeply regret that I will not be able to pass on the rest of my learning to you."

"Yes, that is regrettable." I sighed. Inwardly I didn't care as she did. I thought only about Seneb.

"I don't like important knowledge, which has been passed down for generations, to be lost."

I nodded and swallowed.

"Good night, dear one. Rest well. If you have need of me, please come get me."

"I will, Sister. Good night." And we hugged gently. I could feel her old bones through her white gown. She appeared haggard. Then she left my presence, limping to her room, sandals flip-flopping in the corridor.

That was the last time I spoke to her. She died in her sleep during the night.

Chapter Five

M Y BELOVED SISTER PRIESTESS HENITE was buried deep in the sand outside the Temple complex, in an area with many others that had passed before her. I, and the other girls, and initiates were not allowed to join in the funeral nor the elaborate rituals that accompanied it. One must be an ordained Priestess to be a part of such sacred rites for a Dendera holy woman. I grieved in my small chamber, staying by myself during the day. At night my beloved Seneb visited me. Sorrow was washed away by our impassioned lovemaking.

After Sister had been laid to rest, order was restored to Dendera Temple. I became a Seer for people, rich and poor alike, who visited Dendera for information, advice, or dream interpretation.

I was monitored diligently by other Priestesses, especially Weret-Imtes, to make sure that I made no further mischief. I doubt that anyone could have accurately understood what my misbehavior might consist of. Fortunately, my waywardness was consummated in the dead of night, between me and the energy spirit of a man who lived many miles away, beyond anyone's scrutiny. Seneb, my love.

Notoriety of my valuable intuitive skills began to percolate throughout the area. I was sought after well beyond the local area of Dendera for the messages I received easily and often. Even Dendera Priestesses and initiates as well as Priests from other Temples requested my services. I was delighted and honored to oblige.

Little by little I began to notice that Seneb, the High Priest of Kom-Ombo, visited me less regularly than I would have preferred. I never questioned it, assuming that he had other duties to perform or was tired from his own Temple activities. I eagerly waited for hours in my chamber after everyone was slumbering at Dendera. If he didn't show up at the regular time, I tried to stay awake, in case he showed up late. Thus I developed circles around my eyes and got grouchy from lack of sleep, rare for one as young as me.

When days passed without a visitation, I alternately fretted, cried, and fumed.

When he finally "showed up," I asked him, "Beloved, why do you not visit me oftener as you once did?"

"Did I visit often?" Seneb parried, avoiding answering.

"Yes, of course you did!" I replied hotly. Then assumed a gentler tone, "I believe so."

"Well, I am quite busy as you might know. And sometimes I fall asleep early," he explained impatiently. "Plus there are many more initiates now at Kom-Ombo who require medical training," he added.

"I miss you, my darling," I interrupted.

"Uh, huh," he replied offhandedly. "Well, Kiya, I must go now."

"Must you?" I cried.

"Yes. I cannot stay."

"Why not? When will you come again?" I was frustrated we wouldn't make love that night.

"I'm not sure." Seneb hesitated. "I think I should stop coming to see you, Kiya. It's dangerous for both of us, you know. If we don't stop, it could be only a matter of time before we are found out."

"I'm very careful."

"Yes, but, it only takes one mistake and then I…we…could both be dishonored—or worse."

"My dearest, please don't go," I implored him.

Yet I could feel his Ba disappear. I was left alone on my mattress in the dark. Intuitively I knew that our affair was coming to an end.

Many others took great stock in my intuitions, along with the messages that I obtained so easily. But I refused to believe my own insight about the High Priest and me. I dared not believe, because my menstrual cycle had failed to arrive on time. I was pregnant.

For many nights I attempted to send telepathic messages to the High Priest of Sobek, the man I loved. Perhaps I couldn't channel my communications properly because of my lack of ability. Or else Seneb was blocking me.

My chamber felt heavy with unhappiness and unfulfilled longing. Frustrated, sad and sick with pregnancy, I was distraught. When I wasn't seeing clients, I restlessly wandered around the Temple complex, climbed up the stairs to the roof, paced the roof's perimeter, then walked down the stairs again. Then up to the roof once more, to avoid my lonely room. Being outside in the daylight, in nature, with the blue sky overhead, listening to the sound of ducks and geese in the Temple animal pen, lightened my burden.

I dreaded going back inside when night fell. The silence and emptiness of my room berated me. I had acted like a fool with the High Priest. Seneb obviously didn't care for me. Maybe he had only toyed with me because I was available and eager. I had been powerless over my body, my desire, my love for him. And now I was faced with an even greater humiliation. In due time my dishonor would grow obvious to anyone with eyes. The swollen belly of a wayward, wicked girl.

I lost count of the days since Seneb had last shown himself to me. After everyone was slumbering in the Temple, I reluctantly went to my mattress as well and lay down, trying to sleep. Straining to ignore my thoughts. Attempting to curb the physical sensations that inevitably arose. I listened to the sound of my breath and the cicadas outside.

Abruptly, my lover was there beside me. Overjoyed, I didn't complain to him of my aching desires, my loneliness, my fruitless attempts to reach him. Seneb began stroking me, kissing me. Then he moved his leg between my thighs as he had done so often and began moving against me. He had trained me well. I was immediately throbbing with delight.

Then he stopped. "What is wrong with you?" he demanded of me.

"What do you mean? I'm here. Everything is the same."

"No, it isn't. You are psychic enough, and so am I, to know when change has occurred."

Confused and angered by his complaints, I pulled away. We were connected, so he could feel my distancing as if he was physically next to me.

"Now I know something is wrong," he said. "Tell me, Kiya."

My tongue loosened out of frustration, morning sickness, yearning, and lack of communication. Words came tumbling out, like knocking over an uneven pile of mud bricks. Words attached to strong emotions. I had kept silent long enough. My nature was still that of a willful, volatile girl.

"I'll tell you!" I shouted in my mind to him. "You changed everything in my life! You ruined my vocation as a Priestess! You discredited and humiliated me for your own pleasure! Your own twisted purposes! You impregnated me! You left me alone for nights on end! And now you ask me what is wrong!?" I waited for an answer, panting with righteous indignation.

"You are...pregnant?" he asked soberly.

"Yes," I replied testily.

"So this is what I have been intuiting. I have felt afraid for some time. Wanting to break all contact with you but couldn't bring myself to do so. You will destroy me."

"Hah!" I screeched at him. "What are you saying? You have already destroyed me!"

"Kiya, be still!" he declared. "We need to figure out how to proceed. Let's see. The first thing you need to do is talk to the Priestess in charge of herbs and potions. She will have a remedy to end the pregnancy. And then…"

"What are you talking about?"

"If you had paid closer attention to your studies, you would have known about herbs, including what herbs to take to avoid pregnancy in the first place," he scolded me.

His lecture only inflamed my temper. Yet he had a point. I had to consider the herbal option, for my own sake. However, adrenaline was coursing through my veins and my body was shaking in rage. I struggled to calm myself. "All right. All right. I will do as you say. I will talk to her tomorrow."

"Good." I could practically hear him sigh in relief. Then he added, "Do you remember who she is? Rather short and plump?"

"Of course I remember her. She wasn't very happy at my lack of progress when I studied with her."

With a jolt I realized what information he was withholding. I gasped and my hand flew to my mouth, in total, dreadful, jealousy-ridden comprehension. "Have you been visiting Sitamun at night lately?" I asked. I didn't have to wait for an answer. I knew with certainty he had been with her, just as he had once joined with me. I understood why his visits to me had become irregular. Knew why I was unhappy. "What other Priestess or initiate do you spend each night with?" I cross-examined him viciously. He volunteered no answer.

He closed himself down to me. Shutting himself and his vulnerability away in an untouchable place inside himself, where I couldn't reach him. Did he do that for protection? Security? Out of fear? Indifference? I didn't know. But it hurt.

Chapter Six

I HAD NEVER KNOWN anyone who could completely cut me out of his or her life without a backward glance as Seneb was doing. Sharp as a whetted blade; cruelly indifferent and silent.

With others there was some communication. A look. A flicker of emotion. Words. But not this time. I felt as though I was dead to him. More than dead. As though I had never existed at all. Our irresistible passionate relationship, including the physical and telepathic links, was severed with terrible finality.

I desperately sent mind messages, but got no response. Then I tried to let go of him. I struggled to understand, and prayed to Hathor to accept my fate. But I couldn't let go. A massive, all-consuming, profound connection to him existed beyond my control, possessing me entirely.

I visited Sitamun, the Priestess who had taught me about herbs and herbal medicines. She had already consulted with me several times after I became Seer. Apparently she had forgiven my lack of interest in herbs and was eager to talk with me on both those occasions.

I discovered early in my training that people need to talk about themselves. Sitamun was no exception. Furthermore, as Temple Seer, I realized I enjoyed listening to people as they openly discussed themselves, as they sought information from an extraordinary source with me as messenger. I appreciated that everyone who came to see me needed a sympathetic ear, and trusted me with secrets they didn't dare divulge to anyone else. I didn't betray them, nor did I gossip, while holding their trust as a sacred bond between us. Although I would never be ordained as a Priestess, I thought of myself as one.

Therefore, when I asked Sitamun about herbs to end pregnancy, she was willing to tell me what herbs to use and how to use them. She never asked me if I was the pregnant one. Perhaps she assumed I had come on behalf of a pregnant woman who was afraid to reveal herself. The Priestess offered to make a packet which I could give to the woman in question. Relieved not to answer troublesome questions, I took the packet from her the next day, while I paid close attention to the specific directions involved.

"Is the woman in the early phase of pregnancy?" she asked.

To which I answered, "Yes." Ostensibly the herbs worked most effectively during the first month or two.

I waited until suppertime. No one would miss me until at least the following morning. Hopefully I would have miscarried by then. I made preparations. Filled a large vessel with water. Gathered some clean rags to absorb blood and tissue. Took off my clothes. But although I wanted to end the pregnancy, I could not force myself to consume the potion.

I fumed in frustration. The growing child was the only tangible part of Seneb I had left. I couldn't bear to sever that fragile cord nor to end a new life developing inside me. I cried myself to sleep in irritation, fear, and grief.

Yet within a few days my body elected to terminate the pregnancy of its own accord.

I was "seeing" for a farmer from my home village, who came to ask about both his crops and his wayward wife. We were well into the session. I was receiving unmistakable messages about his wife and her lover, while divulging the precious information to the villager.

Suddenly my belly began to spasm, and I experienced deep, stabbing pain. It didn't take an intuitive to know what was transpiring. I quickly made an excuse to the farmer, and ran from the unadorned room inside Dendera Temple where I held psychic consultations. Blood gushed, running down my legs. I got to my chamber. The water and rags were still where I left them. I grabbed some of the rags and put them within reach. I pulled off my gown and, naked, shakily sat down on the straw mattress.

My abdomen and vagina were cramping violently. I put one clean rag between my teeth and tried not to cry out. Shoved several other rags between my legs to absorb the blood, and lay down, knees bent, feet on the mattress. My heart beat wildly, not knowing what would happen next.

I quickly expelled a huge clot, bled for a while, then the bleeding eventually slowed. I still had occasional abdominal cramps but not as severe as before. By nightfall I was feeling better. I washed myself thoroughly. Walking on unstable legs I went outside near the visitors' quarters, buried the bloody rags deep in the sand, then returned to bed to recuperate. I healed quickly and cleanly, without further problems other than an elongated menstrual period.

No physical link now existed between Seneb and me. Only silence. And my pitiful yearning.

An audacious plan began to form in my mind.

I made preparations. First I would talk to the herbal Priestess Sitamun. Gain her confidence and trust. Become her friend and confidante. Then eventually ply her with questions about the High Priest. I would proceed slowly, to not alarm her, nor hurt or shame her. I simply wanted information.

Eventually, in typical womanly fashion, she was all too happy to share her romantic secret with me. She told me the story about nocturnal visits that bore an uncanny resemblance to my own with Seneb. I found out, however, that she never had a physical encounter. She explained that only the "Ba of a man" came to her and made love to her regularly. Then over time, the mysterious visits stopped.

Now I became dreadfully curious. I wanted to know how far Seneb's net extended. I made friends with and interviewed almost all the Priestesses at Dendera. I skipped the initiates and village girls serving at the Temple, as well as the older Priestesses.

After I completed my detective work, my conclusion was that almost one third of the Priestesses, mostly young ones who were fairly new to Priesthood, had participated at least once, but sometimes more often, in spiritual lovemaking with an unknown, disembodied spirit of a man. A man who appeared to each of them, seduced, and then had sex with them. Seneb.

The High Priest of Sobek apparently craved sexual contact, while seeking out innocent women who would keep his secret intact. All the visitations took place after his initial seduction of me in the Temple. None were physically accomplished except mine. Seneb had educated himself, through me, in seduction that couldn't be traced back to him in any physical manner. No wonder he wanted to end contact with me. I was dangerous, just as he had intuited.

I kept the information to myself, while my love for Seneb was now marred by anger and wounded pride. I wondered how I could gain revenge, to turn the tables on him and make him jealous so he would suffer as I had. An opportunity soon presented itself, so perfect that I fantasized Hathor Herself had set up the scenario for me.

Word of my psychic skills had spread to the Temple of Sobek. I was told that the High Priest of Kom-Ombo had left to consult with some officials far away for a prolonged period of time. Seneb had always denied permission for me to "see" for members of Sobek's Temple but now the High Priest was gone, traveling on Temple business.

I advised a few Priests and initiates of Kom-Ombo that I was available. Word was sent and I was invited to travel to their Temple. I would consult with those who were interested, "seeing" for each of them over the course of a few days. They were apparently eager for my expertise. Afterwards I would return home to Dendera. My plan was diabolically simple and direct.

I traveled by donkey cart, with several Priestess chaperones, to the Temple of Kom-Ombo. The visitors' quarters at that healing Temple was made ready for me and the two women who trekked with me. The moon was beginning to wax full, a most auspicious time for me to "see."

Eleven men and boys over the age of sixteen, including both Priests and initiates, were keen to have individual counseling sessions with me. A special place was set up for me, at the far end of the Temple complex, in a small dark cubicle generally used for consultations with ailing patients. In addition to being a medical school, Kom-Ombo operated a clinic.

Oil lamps were lit inside the compartment and two chairs were placed facing each other. That way I could talk face-to-face with each man individually. The cubicle was mostly private and yet partially public through the open stone doorway. My chaperone Priestesses took turns sitting near the doorway, out of the sun, and out of earshot as well.

I had a general plan of what I would do. Everything would depend on each individual man or boy that I met with. His openness, willingness, but especially his attraction to me was all-important to the success of my scheme. I had brought the amber bracelet with me, the only piece of jewelry I had been allowed to keep after my disgrace. Wearing it lent me courage and most importantly, power. Sexual power learned from Hathor.

The first morning I met in rapid succession with three boys, all initiates, currently training in medicine. They were interested in me, but none felt appropriate. I answered their questions, and one by one they returned to their duties at Kom-Ombo.

After lunch, I went to the visitors' quarters, to rest until the heat of the day passed. Then I was summoned back to the cubicle. There was a young man, a Priest, waiting for his session. When I walked in, I could feel sexual heat immediately rise in him.

And in me.

He squirmed, trying to make himself comfortable in his discomfort and embarrassment, holding his hands in his lap.

I sat, facing him. Looked him directly in the eyes. Smiled slightly. Gauging his reactions. "I am Kiya."

"Ibebi," he replied shyly.

He was somewhat older than me, but I had the upper hand, a wealth of sexual experience, albeit not completely physical. I wondered if I had the resolution, the boldness, to accomplish what I had set out to do.

Perspiration broke out on his brow. Ibebi blushed a deep red.

I knew in that moment, without a doubt, I would select him as part of my plan. I purposefully said nothing. The silence made him even more ill at ease.

Finally I asked him in almost a whisper, so only the two of us could hear. "Ibebi, have you ever laid with a woman?"

"What? Me? No!" he exclaimed in protest. "I'm a Priest and my vow includes celibacy."

"Would you like to?" I interrupted furtively.

He stood up, alarmed, ready to bolt from the cubicle. The bulge under his kilt refuted his protestations.

"Please, Ibebi. Sit down," I encouraged him gently, motioning to the chair he had vacated. "I won't hurt you," I continued in a silken tone. "I promise."

"I can't. I mean, I shouldn't. What are you saying to me?"

I tactfully changed the subject, bringing us back to the session at hand. "I will answer all the questions you have for me. But I will feel more comfortable, and so will you, if you sit down."

"All right then." He sat.

"What would you like to ask me?"

He gulped, then stoked his courage, inspired by my boldness. Looked to the doorway to determine if anyone could hear and stealthily turned to look at me. "Would you…?" He left the question dangling between us.

I knew exactly what he meant and answered indirectly. "Yes. Tonight. After the moon has set. Out in the desert. Away from the visitors' quarters, outside the Temple complex. Be there. I will find you." I stood up and left quickly. Our session was at an end.

I returned to the visitors' quarters, trembling. I washed my face in the small alabaster basin, then sat in the shade of the mud brick building, overwhelmed, guilty, yet excited, too. I wasn't sure which emotion was the most upsetting. How could I feel excited? How could I share intimacies with another man when I loved Seneb?

When summoned for other readings for the rest of the day, I declined, complaining I was overly tired. I ate little at supper and tried to rest, but I was overwrought. The moon took its time setting in the west, while I fidgeted. Finally, with my two companions snoring, and the sky dark, I picked my way to the meeting place. I had scouted the location earlier in the day.

There he was. I could see his outline in the gloom. I took a deep breath, and went over to him. "Hello, Ibebi."

I was a fairly tall woman and he was the same height as me. I put my hand on his broad shoulder. Ibebi shivered in sexual expectation.

I cannot bring myself to tell you the details what happened with Ibebi and me that night. I experienced pleasure as did the young Priest.

Yet I was nervous, filled with self-reproach as well. When we had finished, he was no longer a virgin. He didn't stay to try again but slunk off.

After he left, I returned quietly to our sleeping quarters, washed myself cautiously, and slept uneasily.

Once the Priestesses and I had our morning meal, we returned to the chamber to await the next patron. Another Priest was waiting outside, discernibly impatient. His complexion was very dark and he had a ravenous look in his eyes.

He sat down across from me and leaned forward in anticipation. "I was told about your reading for the Priest Ibebi yesterday," he began without introduction.

In spite of myself, my face became mottled in embarrassment.

He continued in the same conspiratorial tone. "I was wondering if you might do the same reading for me. Tonight. At the same place."

I was trapped in a web of my own deceit.

He smiled a hyena-like smile, all sharp, mean teeth as though he was facing his prey. "By the way I'm known as Zezemonekh." He grinned. "And you're Kiya."

I found my voice. "I'm sorry, Zezemonekh. I don't know what you are talking about. I don't do readings at night."

"But Ibebi told me…"

"You must have been misinformed," I continued, sounding calmer than I felt. "People have a way of exaggerating to impress friends."

The Priest frowned. The smile was gone. Lines between his eyes deepened as he glowered at me.

"Would you send the next person in to see me please?" I asked cordially. "You and I are finished here," I said with finality, gesturing to the doorway. I knew that he would make no trouble, not with my trusty chaperones outside.

Zezemonekh strode to the door, glared at me one last time, and left.

An initiate was shown in next. He was hardly more than sixteen years of age. His face and head were shaved, as was customary. Yet I didn't think that his beard would have been substantial if left to grow. The skin of his face looked soft, as was his dreamy manner. As I tell you about this boy, I may sound as though I'm a jaded old woman. In truth I was younger than he.

"I'm honored to meet you," he spoke first. "I have never met a Priestess before."

"I'm not a Priestess, young man," I replied. "I am simply a servant of Hathor at Dendera Temple."

"Oh, you have not been through training then?" he inquired, although meaning no disrespect.

"Yes, I have had years of training, which ended without merit. So now I am a Seer and live at the Temple with the others."

"I'm sorry if I offended you," he answered politely.

"No, not at all. Shall we start?"

"I would like that very much."

"Hmmmm." I studied him. "What is your name?"

"Diar." He returned my gaze languorously.

This boy was ready for me, although he may not have known it yet. I could feel my heart beat quicker and my breathing deepen, while tingling started of its own accord. I was certainly ready for him. I decided to give him an official reading first, a short one, before I persuaded him to meet me later.

I realized I had misjudged the boy Diar somewhat. He was not as eager as the Priest I met with the day before. Perhaps due to his devotion to Sobek. Finally, however, his carnal appetite was stronger than his devotional one.

He met me later that night. I found him most pleasurable. He learned quickly with me, then explored my body with his own until we were both happily worn out. I smile even now, thinking of him and our guilty tryst.

The afternoon before the three of us from Dendera were to depart for the Temple, I met the last man who had come for a reading. He had trained diligently as a doctor of medicine and held the position of sesh per ankh hem Sobek, a prestigious office at Kom-Ombo. Perhaps only a step or two away from someday being elevated to High Priest of Healing.

"Hello," I greeted him warmly. "Thank you for waiting to see me."

"Not at all," he replied. "You and I have both been very busy the last few days."

I was alert to any double meaning, but found none in his friendly brown eyes. "That is true."

"I wasn't sure if you would have time and energy to See for me. I'm gratified that you can." He stopped for a moment. "You're not too tired, are you?"

"No, I'm not. Thank you," I said. I liked this man. He was gentle and thoughtful.

He bowed low before me. "Please call me Kewab."

"I'm very pleased to meet you. My name is…"

He finished my sentence. "Kiya, Temple Seer of Dendera."

"Yes, that is correct."

Kewab explained that he examined and treated ailing people in the same cubicle I now inhabited temporarily. He seemed somewhat older than Seneb, the High Priest. Kewab was a highly educated man, practicing medicine, consulting with and treating many sick people. He seemed comfortable in my presence, neither awed nor superior.

"Have you been at Kom-Ombo a long time?" I asked him.

"Yes, since I was a boy of about eight or nine," Kewab replied. "Many years have passed."

"Mmm. I went to Dendera at about the same age, from a village near there."

"I thought you contracted with the Temple as a Seer?"

"It's a long story." I didn't want to discuss my sordid past with him. Not now. Not ever. He would be repulsed.

"Must be an interesting story," he commented. "You seem like a fascinating person, although I hardly know you. I wish you would trust me enough to share your tale."

I unexpectedly broke into tears, the hardness of my vengeful plan melting in his benevolent presence.

Kewab rose and came to my side, concerned. "Did I say something wrong? Did I insult you in some way?"

"No," I wept. "Just the opposite."

He took hold of my hand and held it, comforting me. His own hand was warm and soothing.

"You don't know me. You wouldn't understand," I added.

"If you mean the stories I have heard about you from several of the inhabitants here? No, I wouldn't believe them."

"There are stories!?" I was horrified and withdrew my hand.

Completely professional now, Kewab the doctor Priest left my side and went to the open doorway to speak to the Dendera Priestess outside, who was guarding the holy space.

"This lady is unwell. I'm going to care for her. You may retire now. Have some supper. Rest for your journey home."

Incredibly, my Priestess chaperone left her post.

Kewab returned, pulling his chair up close to me. "Now that I've met you, I can understand the stories. You are beautiful. And alluring. The men here are without women in their lives, so I could understand they would adore you." He gently wiped tears from my face with his index finger. "Even when you have been crying."

I was astounded, moved by his words and actions. "I've never met anyone like you in my life."

"Nor I you," he replied tenderly.

"Oh, no," I said impulsively. I closed my eyes, unable to look at him anymore. *I must be courageous,* I thought. *Hold myself back.* Then I opened my eyes, unable to resist his sweetness. Not able to lie. "They are not stories. What you have heard about me is true." I confessed.

"Even if the stories are true, the deeds do not discredit you." He leaned very close and whispered, "I would be honored and privileged if those stories included me. I would take that honor to the afterlife as the most magnificent night of my life." He impulsively caressed my lips with the same finger.

"Please, don't," I implored him. "I can't bear it."

"And the stories of the last few days are not all the stories I know of you," he said softly. "I know you were in rigorous training to become the personification of Hathor Herself. A sacred lineage passed down for ages. To you."

"How do you know that?"

"Because you were being trained with my knowledge and approval. You were meant to join with me in due time."

"But…"

"The High Priest. Yes, I know. Seneb intervened. Then your training ended. And you were disgraced. But now I see that you have embodied the golden Neter anyway. No matter that you weren't ordained as Priestess. The two men who were intimate with you here at Kom-Ombo told fabulous tales of what it was like to be with you. Astonishing, miraculous descriptions. I believe them."

I summoned courage to explain. "I cannot get over Seneb. I'm trying to make him jealous. So that he will return to me."

"I'm afraid that won't happen. Seneb won't return to you."

"Why?" My heart missed a beat.

"I just know it. He's a very proud man. Stubborn, too. And wary."

"Wary of me?"

"Wary of being dishonored. Of losing his status."

I leaned my head against the Priest's bare chest, seeking relief from my chaotic emotions. "I'm so unhappy."

"I know you are." He held me gently for a moment, then sat me up. "Not here. Not like this. I'm afraid you'll have to pretend a little longer."

"What do you mean?" I asked wearily.

"I want you to be with me. Tonight. When the moon has set in the west and your guardians are sleeping, I will come to the visitors' quarters to get you. Then I will take you somewhere safe and comfortable for the night. Where the jackals can't find us. I'll be with you, as Hathor ordained, for the first and last time. In secret. In service to Hathor as well as to Sobek."

"Hotep," I said to the kindly man at my side.

"Peace to you as well. Until later." Then he left before he would be missed by others.

Chapter Seven

THE DOCTOR-PRIEST KEWAB came to collect me late that night. I waited outside for him, shivering in anticipation and the chill. Holding my hand, Kewab led me through the darkness to a crumbling building not far from Kom-Ombo Temple, but beyond its sacred precincts. Private, sheltered from snooping eyes and ears.

Inside was a straw mattress with a clean covering and a woven blanket on one side. An oil lamp was lit, sputtering in the night air.

Looking around at our snug retreat, I exclaimed "You have prepared this for me?"

"For us."

"Didn't you take a vow of celibacy?" I asked in surprise.

"Not exactly, Kiya. Although I act as if I had. Most do. It is common practice." Kewab gently removed my dress, folded it, lay it down on a broken stone column. He undressed himself, then took me by my hand and lay down with me on the soft mattress, cradling my head in the crook of his arm. He reached over and pulled the blanket over us.

I nestled against his chest, feeling safe and cherished for the first time since Henite left her body and departed for the Duat.

"I have been briefly with two women in my life," he explained. "I am allowed a wife, if I want one. Now I have her. You, Kiya." He delicately stroked my cheek with his free hand.

His tenderness was awe-inspiring. I had never experienced such loving demonstration except with Sister.

"I wish you could become my real wife. That's what you were being trained for. For us to work together in healing unison, to help sick and unhappy people. Hathor and Sobek." He sighed. "But the situation is too complicated now, even dangerous, for that to be reality. So all we have is tonight. In secret."

"I understand. I will keep this secret."

"I know you will." He kissed me gently on the lips. Then caressed my face, my neck, my breasts.

I stroked the nipples of his bare chest, running my fingers down the indentation between his ribs to his waist, then stopped. His excitement grew.

We were interrupted by a commotion outside.

A group of men bearing torches barged inside the crumbling structure.

"Get up, the two of you! You have defiled all sense of decency." It was Zezemonekh, the hyena-faced Priest.

Kewab stood up in protest and to protect me, but was clubbed over the head. He fell, senseless and bloody, to the ground.

"Are you seeking your revenge on me?" I challenged Zezemonekh, angrily rising to my feet, pulling the blanket around my nakedness. "This man is innocent and has done nothing to you. How dare you…"

"Whore!" Zezemonekh shouted and slapped me across the face with the back of his hand.

I heard ringing in my ears and fell to the gravel beneath me. The blanket fell away. I was exposed.

He stood over me with the bloody club, menacing. Daring me to rise again. "You will accomplish no more evil seduction in this life!" Zezemonekh screeched hoarsely. He grabbed me by the hair and forced me to stand. "Dress yourself." He threw my dress at me.

I hurriedly slipped it on.

"Take her," he motioned to one of the other men in the group. Unlike him, they were not Priests. Perhaps men from a local village.

One of them roughly grabbed my arm and I was led back to Kom-Ombo, stumbling over obstacles in the darkness.

When we had made our way to the Temple, I was brought to a hole in the ground, big enough for one person. What its purpose was, I had no clue. However, I was made to climb into it, then hunkered down on my knees.

"Make sure she stays there," said the snarling Priest, my sworn enemy. Then Zezemonekh departed, leaving the three men guarding me.

I had no idea what my fate might be. The sun Ra rose in the east. I was given no nourishment nor water all day. I tried to make myself comfortable in the small space, sitting cross-legged, then stooping, then squatting. My muscles screamed for relief. My mouth and throat grew parched in the heat. The men ate, drank, joked, all the while ignoring my misery.

"Could you bring me some water?" I croaked.

"The bitch wants some water," one of them snickered to the others. They paid no attention.

By nightfall the men wearied of their task and, without further orders, wandered off.

I crawled out of the pit after they left. I had managed to remain calm all day, but now I was terrified. Confused. Uncertain. My mind could make no sense of my situation or what to do. For a moment I thought of running away, but the Temple was surrounded by vast desert populated with wild animals, crocodiles, and snakes.

The guards had left behind a goatskin of water. I thirstily drank the remains from it. My face felt swollen and sore from where the Priest had struck me. I was hungry, but afraid to wander around, to look for food. I crouched like a hunted animal near the hole, hoping to be invisible, trying to clear my head enough to formulate a plan of escape.

"Do you want to visit your victims now?" I heard a familiar, awful voice behind me. "They are guarded as well. They are guilty, like you. They will be punished just as you will be."

Zezemonekh bent down level with my face. I could see his glittering eyes in the moonlight. "Is it my turn now, Priestess? Oh, that's right. I forgot. You're not a Priestess. You're not even an initiate. You're nothing at all. But you acted superior with me, didn't you? Thought you were better than me. Smarter than me. Who is smarter now?"

"You are," I whimpered, trying to dampen his rage. "Please don't hurt me."

"Hurt you? No, I won't hurt you. Not any more than you hurt me." He pointed at his chest. Then indicated his groin.

"The Priest Kewab. The man you found me with. Is he all right?" I asked meekly.

"Will he live? Is that what you're asking me?"

I nodded.

"Yes, he will recover. But his life as he knew it is over. He will never be allowed to practice medicine any more. He is dishonored and disgraced. Because of you." He pointed his finger at me. It felt like a weapon and I cringed. Then he changed his tone. "Come with me," he hissed, trying to act like a lover but failing.

"Where?"

"To an intimate setting. A little love nest. Made for you and me."

Dread filled me. "Please. Let me return to my chaperones in the visitors' quarters. Let me go back to Dendera."

"Yes," he goaded, toying with me as a cat would play with a bird or a rodent. "You will go back to Dendera. But not quite yet. First you must make atonement to me." He took my arm and pulled me to my feet, dragging me to his lair.

My feet bled from the stones on the ground. My face ached. But no matter.

He had his way with me for hours, expelling his rage onto and into me. Each moment an eternity of torment. No woman should ever experience what I did that night. He wasn't making love to me. Rather he was punishing me.

I prayed to Hathor to let me die. Yet I lived.

Chapter Eight

THE GIRL THAT WAS DELIVERED to Dendera Temple was hardly recognizable to any of its female inhabitants. Her eyes were sunken and glazed over. The short dress she wore was ragged and dirty. Her face and body savaged. Swollen. Bruised. Her spirit broken as well. She spoke not a word. She was led to her chamber, where she was confined. Food and water was left for her but she ate and drank little.

That girl was me.

A tribunal was assembled at Dendera Temple, to investigate "the matter of the Seer and her despicable behavior at Kom-Ombo." To bring judgment against me and my cohorts. Included on the panel to assess my guilt was Seneb and Weret-Imtes. They weren't my friends. Zezemonekh, the man who had discovered me and my plot, then wounded and humiliated me, was called in to witness my actions. He wasn't my friend, either.

Although my crime wasn't a capital one, I was sentenced to death. Perhaps as a means to hush up wrong-doing at the top of the Temple hierarchy. Possibly as revenge. Maybe because I had learned too many sacred mysteries that couldn't be shared outside the Temple. Or more likely to make sure that no one knew the truth about Seneb and me. I would never know for sure the actual reason for the ruling.

The two priests and the initiate from Kom-Ombo—Ibebi, Diar and Kewab—fortunately did not suffer the same consequence I did. They were dismissed from the Temple of Sobek and lived the rest of their lives in disgrace—but alive. I never saw any of them ever again.

On a brilliantly sunny day, I was led in ritual by Priests of Kom-Ombo and Priestesses of Dendera, with much chanting, rattling of sistrums, and solemn demeanor, to the holy mountain. Our distant destination was above an ancient sacred site, which had been in ruins for as long as anyone remembered. Its ancient columns mere broken granite stumps.

Seneb, the High Priest of Sobek, was noticeably absent from the procession. Apparently pressing business kept him at Kom-Ombo that day.

All of us climbed the steep precipice with effort, shuffling through the loose gravel, breathing hard with the elevation as well as the intense heat.

Once at the top, my judgment was repeated for all to hear.

"Kiya, former Temple Seer, is to be punished for her wrong-doing. In the name of Ma'at and justice."

A young Priest was designated to push me over the side of the cliff, carrying out my death sentence. As he stepped behind me, he mumbled with regret in his voice and demeanor, "I'm sorry to have to do this. Please forgive me."

"I do forgive you," I told him.

My life was finished anyway. If I lived, Seneb, my beloved High Priest, would never return to me. I'd be homeless as well, dispelled from the Temple. An outcast, my family and village would never be allowed to speak to me after the disgrace I had brought upon them.

Just then a strong wind came up, blowing everyone's robes around them. On the ground far below, the sand made swirling patterns in the gusty air.

I stood facing out toward the edge of the cliff. I felt strangely remote, as though my life had been merely a story I had made up. A disturbing fairy tale that was now at its end.

Memories of Seneb and my adoration for him flickered through my mind, like moths hovering around a torch. Physical pain of longing and desire filled me. Missing him, as a babe, hungry and wailing, would yearn for its mother's breast. Aching sensations rose in me, stinging my eyes. As though my heart had been violently ripped from my chest, lying bloody at my feet. A gaping hole not to be filled again. I had no anger nor revenge left in me. Only grief.

Abruptly the young Priest gave me a hard shove.

In the instant before I fell to my death, my last thoughts were of Seneb. I died loving him as fiercely as I always had.

While our karma had become dreadfully unbalanced.

Part Two:

Chapter Nine

THE YEAR WAS 1990 A.D., and I was in love with Saul, a married man. He had left his wife and a home in England to live with me in California. Although we had dated for months, when we moved in together, our relationship became troubled. Whether it was his grief for leaving his life and his wife, or for some other reason, our relationship had soured. The stress of living under the same roof was unbearable.

Although he had given up his former existence to be with me, Saul was reluctant to make a commitment to a permanent relationship. "I'm so much older than you," he explained. "You should find a young man to be with."

"But I love you." I countered. Your age doesn't make any difference to me."

He seemed unconvinced.

I didn't know how to resolve the situation nor the recent unease that had rose between us.

So I left Saul, who continued to live in my apartment, while I moved to a house belonging to two professors at the University. The Smythe's were going on sabbatical leave to study overseas, and needed a house sitter. They asked if I was available.

"Yes," I readily agreed.

Saul and I still cherished each other. We continued to talk to, and see each other, almost every day. Fortunately we had a few months to work out the difficulties in our relationship before the Smythe's were expected to return.

One fateful afternoon my friend Linda came to visit me. She currently lived in Arizona, so we were enjoying each other's company, catching up with our lives. Elaine, a mutual friend of ours, happened to call.

"You'll never guess," I told her. "Linda is here visiting."

"I'll be right over!" Elaine immediately drove over, bringing her boyfriend Clooney with her.

Linda and I were overjoyed to have Elaine join us. We all hugged each other on first sight.

In her excitement Elaine didn't introduce either of us to Clooney. Elaine and Linda headed for the living room, chattering and laughing, apparently forgetting about the two of us standing at the front door of the Smythe's house.

When I turned to Clooney, I noticed the etched lines around his upturned mouth, intriguing in an enigmatic way. He was taller than me. Older but in great physical shape, and dressed in stylish casual clothes.

His nonchalant smile hit me like a blow to my solar plexus. He silently studied me with his feline green eyes. He reminded me of a cougar. He tilted his head to one side and looked at me from the corners of his slanted, half-closed eyes. They were the sexiest eyes I had ever seen. Bedroom eyes, they're called. His gaze was insistent and insolent. Taunting me. Teasing me. Encouraging me.

I felt faint, as though falling from a great height. My body felt like it had been blasted open by a stroke of lightning streaming through me, supercharging me. Instantly altering my reality into something alien, yet enormously inviting and pleasurable. Like nothing I had ever experienced before. Certainly not with Saul.

My sex drive screamed into high gear. My body grew outrageously physical as if I had become a feral animal in heat. Or maybe I always had been wild, but with Clooney, my desire was released from captivity. I was blazing with wanton fever.

I yearned for us to throw off our clothes. To lay down on the faded red carpet in the hallway between the Smythe's musty bookcases. Make love together on the spot. Intertwine our bodies like a caduceus.

My breathing intensified. My heart pounded so hard I thought it would burst out of my chest. Every cell of my body was aflame with delicious sensations. Prickles of goose bumps raised up on my skin. My clitoris, vulva, and breasts ached for his touch. I wanted to touch him. Kiss his smiling lips. Lick him. Fuck him.

Instead...I did nothing.

As the two of us stood frozen to the spot, never breaking eye contact, I recognized him. Remembered him, although we had never met before. As if we were reunited after a long disruption of time and place. Igniting an Immortal partnership. Finding ourselves again in undying adoration.

In that moment I fell in love with Clooney. He stared at me, as though he recognized me as well. The pupils of his eyes dilated. He seemed as overwhelmed with sexual desire as I was. He continued to stare at me, his upturned mouth smiling an invitation.

He reached past me and closed the front door I had forgotten about. He moved closer, then deliberately rested his sizzling hand on my arm. I jumped as if I had been electrocuted and he backed away. My arm smoldered and quivered where he had touched it.

My head swam with an impossible idea. I wanted to run away with him. Immediately. To leave everything and everyone behind. My job.

Home. Everything I owned. My two friends were forgotten in the other room. Saul was a few miles away, probably thinking of me, but I would willingly abandon him as well. Nothing and no one else existed in the world for me but Clooney. I was willing to die of bliss in his arms.

Recognizing instantly the hopelessness of my thoughts and feelings, with immense effort I brought myself back to painful reality. I wanted to keep him at my side, in private, together, for as long as possible. What I actually desired couldn't be fulfilled, but I didn't want to release him. Not just yet.

"Would you like a tour of the house?" I asked him. An absurd question under the circumstances.

"Sure," he replied inanely.

I showed Clooney around the house I was caring for. I chatted about ridiculously mundane matters, in order to maintain a semblance of connection between us. All was pretense and he knew it, but he willingly accepted the subterfuge.

My spatial acuity was distorted by desire. My mind had melted, not able to reason. I bumped into walls. Crashed into furniture. Always aware that Clooney was only an arm's length away from me.

Clooney and I toured the Smyth's personal office.

"Here's their matching desks," I reported.

"Uh huh," Clooney replied, feigning interest in a stapler on one desk with exaggerated care.

"And their computers."

"Uh huh."

We made eye contact almost continuously. Our eyes made love while our bodies screamed silently. Our minds raced. We could hardly breathe in the electric tension surrounding us.

Just then Linda and Elaine sought us out.

Linda announced, "We're starved. Let's go eat. Elaine's going to drive us to Rutabagorz. Come on."

We all piled into Elaine's black BMW. Linda sat in the front seat to continue her engrossing conversation with Elaine. That meant that Clooney and I were cast together in the back seat.

Clooney was an extremely playful as well as an intensely amorous man. On the way to the restaurant he tickled me relentlessly, and I tickled him in return. We had mock wrestling matches, now touching each other with abandon, pretending it was accidental. We giggled like two kids, squirming and wriggling happily in the back seat of Elaine's car, finally having reasons to touch each other.

In a logical, but temporarily inaccessible, part of my mind, I was horribly embarrassed for behaving shamelessly with Elaine's boyfriend. I couldn't help myself. In the nanosecond during which I met him, I emerged fully alive, impassioned, on fire around Clooney, in a way I had never experienced with anyone else before or since. I couldn't, didn't want to stop the feelings. Furthermore, I found it painful to take my hands off him. Agony to move apart. He and I sat side by side in the restaurant, our bodies pressed against each other. Elaine didn't seem to notice.

The rest of the evening was a blur. Somehow I ate. I was dropped off at the Smythe's house…alone. I couldn't sleep or rest or sit still.

Clooney called me every day for a week. We talked and flirted, made overtly provocative suggestions to each other, incinerating the phone wires. I adored him. I couldn't get enough of him. His voice. His deeply passionate energy. His playful sensuality.

But I still had Saul to consider. I am pathologically honest, so I told Saul about what was transpiring between Clooney and me.

Saul was alarmed. He made an outrageous suggestion, although at the time it seemed appropriate.

"I don't know any way to compete with your fantasy about him. So invite him over. We'll have a three-some and that will take care of your daydream for him once and for all."

Have sex with the two men I loved? I could hardly contain my excitement at the mere idea. Why wait?

Immediately I telephoned Clooney. "Saul and I would like you to come over to his apartment tomorrow night."

"Okay," Clooney agreed. Without hesitation. Without question.

When Clooney arrived, the three of us sat in the living room and talked. Clooney had no idea—or maybe he did—of what Saul and I were thinking. Saul and Clooney had a lot in common (in addition to me) and they talked together for over an hour, enthusiastically becoming acquainted. I observed their relating with curiosity—and some relief.

Then Saul changed the subject. "Why don't we go to bed now?" as if it was the most natural suggestion in the world. He led the way, Clooney followed, and I walked behind the two men.

Sexy words and phone calls were all right as far as fantasy was concerned. But now I was faced with reality. Shy and hesitant, I removed my clothes and got into bed. Then Clooney and Saul did the same and lay down on either side of me.

What was I to do? Who to kiss first? How to touch one without ignoring the other? How could I focus on Clooney while turning my back on Saul? Although the daydream of making love to two men had always intrigued me, the protocol was confusing. Fantasy far outweighed reality.

After we had stroked each other and kissed for a while, Clooney got dressed and went home.

Once alone with me, Saul cried out. "I don't want to share you with anyone!" he announced. "I want you to be with me exclusively."

That was Saul's declaration for a primary relationship with me.

I agreed. The next day I called Clooney. "I'm sorry. I'm breaking off contact with you," I told him. "Please don't call me again. I'm going to be in a monogamous relationship with Saul. I love him very much."

The truth was I loved both of them, but had to make a decision.

Clooney sounded sad. "Okay. I wish you well."

Nine years passed without contact with Clooney. I thought about him, missing him and our intense connection. Eventually he receded to the back burner of my awareness, on simmer.

In time Saul and I moved in together. My relationship with him developed, grew, and deepened. We had good times and difficult ones, like any other couple. We bought a house together and moved to Corona. Then we rented out our house and moved back to Fullerton, near his work at the University.

Saul and I traveled extensively. It was then that I received a psychic message to go to Egypt.

Chapter Ten

DURING A MEDITATION in 1996 I received a vision of an ancient Egyptian woman with a huge golden headdress who told me: "Go to Egypt."

I then met with a new friend, Delores, who showed me exquisite photos of her recent trip to Egypt.

When she displayed her photos of Dendera, I got goosebumps. "Dendera? What is Dendera?" I asked her.

"I think it's a healing temple," Delores explained. "They also trained priestesses to be psychic and interpret dreams."

"I have to go to Dendera!" I announced. I always trust my gut feelings. I had been a healer and psychic most of my life, so it felt right.

I researched online and found only one metaphysical tour that included Dendera—Ancient Tours—and I signed up immediately. Saul declined, saying he wasn't interested in Egypt.

When I arrived in Giza at the fabulous 4-star Mena House Hotel overlooking the Pyramids, I met Ancient Tours' owner, Mohammed. We felt like instant friends and hugged with delight. Then he handed me an itinerary.

After perusing the itinerary thoroughly, I exclaimed, "Where's Dendera?! Aren't we going to Dendera?"

"No, we had to cancel that portion of the trip. It requires an army convoy and we couldn't arrange it in time," Mohammed clarified.

"But I have to go! It's why I joined your tour. Can I take a bus or train—a camel—or something?" I asked.

"I'm sorry," Mohammed explained. "It's an impossible journey on your own. Because of the danger of fundamental Islamists, tour regulations require an army convey escort tourists to that area."

I was dejected.

The next day our tour group visited the Great Pyramid complex in Giza. Impulsively I put my third eye against a huge stone block on the ground level of the Great Pyramid. Suddenly I was in a vision: I was flying through stars in the cosmos. I landed on earth. I found myself in a dark, low, narrow enclosed walkway. It curved to the right. There was a tiny doorway with steps leading down. To what?

I rushed over to Mohammed to ask him what he thought my vision meant.

"That's Dendera," he said meaningfully.

"Oh, now I REALLY need to go to Dendera!" I exclaimed. "Are you sure there's no other way?"

Mohammed shook his head. "No, there isn't."

Several days later our group toured the Cairo Museum. In front was a large lotus pond with papyrus. I wept seeing it, not knowing why.

I wandered away from the group and found the King Tut exhibit. The items were beautiful but didn't stir my emotions. Next to it was the ancient jewelry exhibit. I went inside, looked at the jewelry and burst into tears again. I'm sure everyone must have thought I was an odd tourist, crying over old jewelry.

A few days later we flew south to Luxor. At dinner I saw our American tour guide whispering to Mohammed. I sensed that meant we were going to Dendera. After dinner, Mohammed announced, "We are going to Dendera tomorrow!"

I hugged Mohammed in gratitude.

When we arrived at Dendera, I hurried through the crumbling mud brick entrance. The magnificent Hathor columns of the Temple rose before me. Dendera was Hathor's Home, the golden woman I had first seen in my meditation, who had instructed me to "GO TO EGYPT." I prostrated myself on the dusty ground. I was home.

The group went off with our assigned Egyptologist to view Dendera's Temple and grounds. I couldn't wait. I started exploring the many acres, looking for my vision.

Every time I stopped to gather my thoughts, an Egyptian man came up to me. He was dressed in Western clothes so I knew he wasn't a temple guard, as they always wear a galabaya robe.

When I stopped, the man told me, "You need to see the crypt."

I waved him away, saying, "No, thanks. I'm looking for something." Besides I had been warned not to go off with Egyptian men, because they took "liberties" with Western women.

Then I would rush off in a different direction, still followed by the Egyptian man. I got discouraged and went to find Mohammed. He was up on the roof of the Temple. "Mohammed, where is my vision?" I asked him.

"I think it is over by the sacred lake," he replied, pointing to the now-dry lake enclosed by palm trees.

I raced over to the sacred lake, down some stairs, and looked into all the cubicles I saw there. Nothing. My vision was nowhere to be found.

The man came up to me again. "You need to see the crypt."

I was exhausted and frustrated. "Okay," I agreed. "Take me to the crypt."

We went into the massive Temple, with a forest of Hathor pillars standing like sentinels. The persistent man led me to a small dark room with uncarved walls. He went over to a grate, lifted it up, turned on an electric switch and motioned to me. I was supposed to climb into a hole in the ground with an unknown Egyptian man? I decided to do it, since I couldn't find what I was looking for. He helped me down the ladder.

At the bottom of the ladder I was now in the location of my vision. I walked along a dark, low, narrow enclosed walkway, which curved to the right. There was a tiny doorway with steps down—to the crypt.

We crawled through the doorway and made our way down to a beautiful limestone series of chambers, carved with elegant figures, designs, and hieroglyphics. I said a quick prayer. Did a short meditation. Then took some snapshots while the Egyptian man stood unobtrusively to the side.

When I was done, he asked, "Do you know what the crypt was used for?"

"No." I laughed. "I didn't even know there was a crypt here."

The Egyptian man continued. "The crypt is where the sacred jewelry was stored."

Suddenly everything became quite clear. I now knew I had lived at Dendera before. I had taken care of, or at least knew about, the sacred jewelry.

He held out his hand for me to shake. "My name is Mohammed. I work for Ancient Tours in this part of Egypt." Mohammed smiled. "I grew up in this area, in Qena, close to this Temple. I used to play here all the time as a kid. Then I grew up, went to University, and became an Egyptologist. I work for the Luxor Museum. I don't usually talk to people in Mohammed's tour groups. I take care of details. But then I saw you get off the bus and I knew I had to take you to see the crypt."

I was breathless with awe. The universe had gone through amazing gymnastics to create this series of synchronicities.

Mohammed continued. "You're a daughter of Hathor, aren't you?" He gazed at the 18K gold Hathor pendant necklace I was wearing, having bought it the day before in a Luxor jewelry shop.

"I'm not sure what you mean. But, yes, I think I am," I replied.

"You've lived here before."

"Yes, I believe I have."

"I mean, before now. I knew you then." I understood what he meant. The young man was telling me he was acquainted with me in a previous life.

I told him my whole story, including the vision I had at the Great Pyramid. "How did you know to bring me to the crypt?"

He shrugged. "I recognized you when you got off the bus. From… before…I realized you needed to see the crypt."

My mind was in a whirl. No logical thoughts prevailed. Only an immense feeling of joy, a sense of homecoming, along with gratitude in trusting my messages, visions, and intuitions. And gratitude for Mohamed bringing me to the crypt.

As if in a trance, I murmured to him, "I'm a writer. I'm going to write a book about this Temple someday."

Mohammed shyly added: "Many people have asked me to help them write their books about Dendera. I've always said no." He paused, and then continued. "But I will help you."

Not feeling like strangers any more, I hugged Mohammed from Qena.

When I returned to California, I valiantly tried to stay in touch with Mohammed, who had taken me to the crypt. Phone calls were impossible then. Hardly anyone had cell phones. I called his mother's home, but no one spoke English there. Letters disappeared into the void of a third world country postal system. I returned to Egypt twice, but Mohammed was out of the country both times. I never saw him again.

Chapter Eleven

URING THE SAME TOUR that I encountered Dendera, our group was scheduled to go to Karnak, an immense temple complex covering many acres, built and added to over centuries by many Pharaohs.

A buzz went around our group when Mohammed, owner of Ancient Tours, announced that we would be having a private showing inside the Ptah sanctuary, including a very-famous statue of Sekhmet.

I confess to my almost-total ignorance at that time. Prior to this first trip I knew virtually nothing about Egypt, limited to the Giza complex with its pyramids and sphinx—Isis, Osiris, Ramses the Great, and Cleopatra. So when the name Sekhmet was introduced, I shrugged, not understanding the excitement.

When the tour arrived at Karnak, I was overwhelmed by the immensity of the place. I could have easily gotten lost, so I stuck close to our group. And of course I didn't want to miss the private viewing of the enigmatic Sekhmet.

It was late morning and the temperature had soared to 127°. I drank water non-stop and my legs were swollen from the heat, but I doggedly followed the others. Emil, our group's Egyptologist, led the way to the sanctuary of Ptah. We had to wait for a prior group to finish their time inside, so we waited in whatever shade we could find.

Finally it was time to go inside. A quiver of excitement passed through me as we entered the tiny sanctuary. Inside was quite dark, lit only by a small opening in the ceiling. The granite walls were bare of decoration. In the middle of the small space was the black basalt statue of the Neter Sekhmet light from the hole in the ceiling illuminating her.

Sekhmet, with her stylized lioness head and larger-than-life-sized body of a woman, was placed on a granite dais. Including the sun disk over her head, she stood well over seven feet tall. I had to look up to see her eyes. She was holding a carved ankh, the key of life, in one hand, and a Was scepter in the other.

To say she was commanding is an understatement. Sekhmet took my breath away.

We had been advised throughout our travels in Egypt to avoid touching any of the antiquities, to maintain their condition for future generations. Yet at this sanctuary we were not only allowed, but encouraged, to touch Sekhmet. Emil showed us the ritual of touching her. Each of us was instructed to touch the top of Sekhmet's head, then our head. Then touch her heart and our heart. Finally we were asked to move aside to allow the next person in line to do the same ceremony.

We lined up single file in front of Sekhmet. When my turn came, I dutifully did as Emil had demonstrated. Her head, my head. Her heart, my heart. Then I stepped aside, to stand next to her. I reached out to touch Sekhmet's arm. It was chilly to the touch, especially after the blazing heat outside. I stroked it, amazed at both the coolness and smoothness of the basalt.

Suddenly—without warning—I felt the arm move under my hand. Then the statue turned and looked at me.

Her gaze was kindly, almost motherly, yet compelling and powerful. Involuntarily I screamed. Statues are not supposed to move. Then I hurried outside.

I stood trembling in the courtyard of the sanctuary of Ptah, wondering if I had lost my senses, or was it the heat? Did I imagine it? Sekhmet's moving arm felt real beneath my hand and yet...

Several women from our group joined me outside. They were grinning at me.

One of them said, "That was amazing!"

"What was amazing?" I asked coyly, wanting verification, without exposing myself to ridicule.

"The statue. She turned and looked at you."

"You saw it?"

"Yes," the woman continued. "But that isn't all. The most amazing thing was when Sekhmet turned and looked at you, a light came out of her head and entered your head."

"What?!" I exclaimed. "Oh, my goodness, what does this mean? Did she do that to you, too?" I asked her.

"No," the woman said dejectedly. "Just you."

The other woman nodded her head yes in agreement. I, alone, had been selected for the Neter's gaze that day, a metaphorical "tap on the shoulder."

I made a mental note that when I returned home I needed to research this lion-headed being whose statue could move. Who was Sekhmet? Why did she do that? What did she want from me? I wouldn't have long to wait.

Meanwhile, Emil, our tour group's Egyptologist, teased me incessantly during the rest of the tour about my becoming Sekhmet.

I had been back from my metaphysical tour in Egypt for a week. I was dressed and standing in front of my mirror, applying make-up, preparing to go out. Unexpectedly Sekhmet appeared in the upper left corner of the mirror, looking as she had in Ptah's sanctuary, only alive now, not a statue.

"I have chosen you," she told me clearly, without introduction.

Then she continued. "I want you to return to Egypt as soon as possible, buy merchandise, and start a store."

I doubt anyone argues with Sekhmet, yet I couldn't help myself. "But…I'm a terrible salesperson and I can't run a business," I tried to explain to her.

"This is not about making money," Sekhmet continued, undeterred. "I want you to bring Egypt to people who are interested."

"Okay," I agreed reluctantly, assuming correctly she meant I was to buy ancient Egyptian reproductions to sell to interested people around the world. I would have been better off giving items away as I lost a lot of money in the seven years I ran my business. Sekhmet was right in saying it wasn't about making money. But life with Sekhmet would turn out to be quite an adventure, and worth a fortune.

I consulted the internet for information about Sekhmet.

Everything I read about her was terrifying. Goddess of Wrath. Blood-thirsty. Ferocious. Avenger for her father Ra towards non-believers. Drinking their blood in a frenzied rage, unable to stop murdering people until Thoth tricked her with red beer and she got drunk.

Drunken Sekhmet then went to sleep and awoke as Hathor—so the legend goes. Where was the motherly lioness who looked at me so fondly in Egypt? And the Sekhmet in the mirror who gave me orders, but not in a frightening way. Rather like a mother lion nudging her young cub in the direction she wanted it to go.

I decided to trust my own experiences and intuitions with Sekhmet, rather than relying on what I read. I'm glad I did. The Sekhmet I knew and loved is not like the awful stories from the Internet. Nowadays, many other people are having positive, albeit challenging, experiences with the lioness Neter, so I feel vindicated.

I then contacted Mohammed from Ancient Tours, to find out when his next metaphysical tour was scheduled.

He was pleased to hear from me. "The next tour is a special one," he told me with excitement. We are having a number of famous guest writers traveling with us, lecturing as well as conducting a symposium." I signed up at once and five months later I was back in the bosom of Mother Egypt.

Before I went to Egypt the second time, Sekhmet spent months teaching me. She informed me she was primarily a Neter of creation, not destruction. That creation comes into being from the unformed universe through a combination of desire and passion, similar to the big bang. She especially taught me to "hold the energy" so that my own creativity would be enhanced through withheld desire and passion. That meant I would have to refrain from sexual activity with Saul. It wasn't easy. But I did it.

Chapter Twelve

MY FRIEND ELAINE HAD trained to teach a new age course on self-discovery. She invited me to attend the seven-day workshop. I accepted. I was her first and only student at the time. Elaine was gratified at the progress I made under her guidance.

I was experiencing profound passion and sexual excitement but had no outlet. Sekhmet was instructing me to "hold the energy" of my sexuality. This meant that I was not allowed to have sex.

Although I loved Saul and we had a pleasant sex life up to that point, I didn't experience romance nor sensuality with him, and certainly not passion.

Vast sexual energy continued to flow through and build in me. The intensity was growing. How much sexual excitement could one body contain? Plus I craved passion.

After I finished Elaine's workshop, Saul decided he was going to take the course, too. He signed up along with several other students.

The first night he arrived home for dinner after the day's workshop, "You'll never guess who's also a student." he announced.

I couldn't guess.

"Clooney," he revealed.

Clooney! I felt panicky. I never recovered from loving and desiring Clooney. Not to mention I was overpoweringly, sexually turned on every waking minute. Not a good combination.

Clooney and Saul hit it off during the basic workshop, picking up from where they had left off as acquaintances years ago during our unsuccessful threesome. The two men then decided to participate in the advanced 10-day training together in San Francisco as roommates.

Every night Saul called me from the hotel, to check in with me and say hello. He kept me up to date on the progress of the workshop, as well as his burgeoning friendship with Clooney. After each day's seminar, Saul and Clooney toured the city, ate at wonderful restaurants, and talked incessantly. The two men became so close many people thought they were brothers.

As their relationship deepened, I became ever more worried. "What will I do if I see Clooney?" I wondered. Saul was safe, but Clooney was dangerous.

Both Saul and Clooney were theoretical thinkers and loved to discuss and debate many subjects. Philosophy. Psychology. Consciousness. Literature. Even god. Saul invited Clooney to sit in on his lectures at the University.

Clooney happily attended. Since Clooney was far from his home in Glendale, Saul invited him to have dinner at our house after each class.

I tried to appear nonchalant during those dinners. Frankly I was walking on eggshells, afraid to make eye contact with Clooney or participate in discussions. Often after the meal I would excuse myself quickly and go to our bedroom, where I'd hide out from temptation. The men continued their conversations for hours. Before it got too late, Clooney would drive home to Glendale, where he lived with his wife Valerie.

Years before, when our relationship first ignited, I didn't know Clooney was married. He had many affairs during his many years with

Valerie, including Elaine and, briefly, me. When he had been a single man, between marriages, Clooney had countless affairs as well. He adored women. And they were mad about him in return. He was a delightfully sexy, sensual, playful man and easily attracted females.

The last night that Clooney went to a class, Saul invited him not only to stay for supper but to sleep over, to put off the long drive home to Glendale until morning. Clooney set down his overnight bag in the guest room. Then he joined us in the dining room.

Shortly after we finished dinner, Saul excused himself. "I'm tired. I'm going to bed," he declared, and left Clooney and me in the living room.

I had been relaxing in my easy chair, ready to excuse myself again. Saul's hasty departure mystified me. I was speechless. I couldn't look at Clooney. I fidgeted, hesitant. To make matters more complicated, I was uncontrollably and intensely turned on sexually.

Clooney came over, sat on the floor next to me, and began to stroke my bare foot. I didn't know until that moment how fright and passion could exist in the same moment.

His touch was a seemingly simple gesture. But it underscored that he was still interested in me. Had he also acted casually during those dinners as I did? Patiently biding his time until he could be alone with me?

Desire leaped from his hand into my foot and then exploded into the rest of my body. I throbbed and quivered at his touch. The experience reminded me of years ago, our first meeting at the Smythe's house.

When his hand moved to my leg, I jumped up from the chair. I couldn't control myself any more. If I stayed I would make a fool of myself and damage my relationship with Saul. Clooney was beyond dangerous. My life would be destroyed.

"Good night," I announced.

"Are you going to bed?" he inquired slyly, his Cheshire cat smile playing around his lips.

"Yes." I bolted from the room. When I had closed the door to our bedroom, undressed and gotten into bed, I realized Saul was still awake. He was privy to what had transpired between Clooney and me in the living room. Had he deliberately set those wheels in motion? If he had, towards what end?

"Are you in love with him?" Saul asked directly.

I couldn't answer his question. No words seemed safe at that moment. My life and future hung hazardously in the balance.

Clooney left our house without spending the night, without even saying goodbye.

Saul didn't hear from him, nor did Clooney attend Saul's classes any more.

I was relieved. And disappointed. I couldn't stop obsessing about Clooney. Desiring him. I was miserable and conflicted.

When I awoke one morning a month later, a decision had been reached. Not by conscious volition, but through some mysterious guidance. I decided to call Clooney, to tell him I loved him. That I wanted to be with him. To find out if he wanted to be with me. I knew my life would shatter into a million pieces if I did so. Yet I knew I couldn't avoid this step.

When I explained my decision to Saul, he was dejected but seemed to understand. He probably understood more than I did.

"I'm worried that I'll eventually lose both of you," I confessed.

Later that day I gathered my courage and resolve, and called Clooney.

He wasn't surprised. He acted as though he knew I would call. He sounded excited. "I'll come over tomorrow and we'll take a drive."

I didn't know what karma we were creating, but the universe had to appreciate our patience of almost ten years.

"Oh, one more thing," I added.

"Yes, sweetie, what's that?"

That was the first time he ever called me sweetie. I loved that he called me an endearment. I loved his voice. I was crazy about him. "I don't want to be a dirty little secret," I said. "I won't be with you unless your wife knows about us."

Surprising me, he readily agreed. The next day, after he picked me up, he drove us to his house in Glendale.

Clooney had an old station wagon with a bench seat. I buckled the middle seat belt, and cuddled up close to him during the long drive. Our hands were all over each other while he drove. I was in bliss.

When we got to his house, he announced our arrangement to his wife Valerie while I listened quietly. She didn't act surprised or angry.

Thus began our training period under Sekhmet.

Chapter Thirteen

AFTER CLOONEY CONFESSED his affair to Valerie, with me as witness, he drove the two of us to a local airport that catered to small planes. He explained that he had flown airplanes for a few years and was still fascinated by them, although he no longer was an active pilot.

He parked his two-toned station wagon in the almost-empty parking lot. We sat and watched many planes take off and land. Cessna, Piper, Beechcraft, and infrequently a private jet. He never took his hands off me nor did I take mine off him. We kissed for prolonged periods, unconcerned that others might be watching us.

With great difficulty I decisively moved away from him to the other side of the front seat. I explained that, because of Sekhmet's rules of "holding the energy," we were not allowed to do anything except touch each other in non-sexual areas (like shoulder or arm or hand) and kiss. Because I was studying to be ordained as priestess of Hathor as well as deepening my knowledge of the Egyptian mystery school, I took Sekhmet's rule seriously.

That afternoon I learned quickly, while sitting for hours in his car in the airport parking lot, how much I adored kissing him. We spent hours that day and many others "holding the energy." How we accomplished Sekhmet's decree without becoming crazed by unconsummated sexual desire, I don't know.

We returned to that airport many times. Visited parks. A nearby lake. Took long drives. Each time we became ever more driven by our passion, yet only kissed and touched so-called innocent body parts.

After every excursion, he returned me to the house I shared with Saul. Then he drove back home to Valerie.

Our love affair was out in the open. Both Saul and Valerie knew and neither made demands nor restrictions on us. Astonishingly, the four of us became friends and spent time together.

Months went by. I was ordained in a special ceremony as a priestess of Hathor under the sponsorship of the worldwide Fellowship of Isis. I was also studying with my hierophant teacher on ancient Egypt mystery school wisdom once a week, learning rituals and chants. I continued to market Egyptian items from my business at both fairs and online. Yet, without a doubt, my favorite occupation was spending as much time as possible with Clooney, while we practiced "holding the energy."

One afternoon the karmic wheel rotated a notch.

Clooney visited me at my house. Saul was gone that day, teaching his classes at the University. Unexpectedly Sekhmet informed me that we didn't have to "hold the energy" anymore. We were free to become lovers and consummate our relationship. Sekhmet told us we had to perform a special, sacred ceremony to her first, to purify ourselves. Which we did.

Unwilling to wait another second to be with each other, we feverishly pulled each other's clothes off, and had unstoppable, unfettered sex on the floor of my living room. That was our first time completely unrestricted and uninhibited, we felt our connection at deep physical levels. We sampled every sexual act we had been prohibited from performing. I believed Sekhmet was smiling at our union.

Afterwards, I no longer could tolerate living in the house I shared with Saul. I wanted to remain free and open with Clooney. To frolic, to experience the fullness and ardor of our union in a private love nest, which required that I move to my own space.

When I told Saul I was moving out, he was upset and angry, but only temporarily. He was a loving, kind man and forgave me quickly, once the shock wore off. We stayed in touch and remained friends.

Then a creative idea materialized. I could rent an apartment and transform part of it into an Egyptian temple. I found an affordable two-bedroom apartment. One bedroom would be for me, with Clooney visiting as often as he could. The other would be an office, where I kept my computer and stored inventory from my store.

The living room and dining area would be transformed into a small-scale temple, complete with altar, statues, papyrus, and other artifacts, all reproductions from my store, of course.

I bought a red futon (Sekhmet's favorite color) for the living room floor, without a frame. Thinking optimistically, the futon would come in handy for future students.

Clooney helped me move my meager possessions to my new home/temple. We baptized the temple area by having sex on the new futon in front of the altar. After all, Sekhmet was the Neter of passion and she was connected to both of us. Hathor, for whom I was ordained, was Neter of romance, sexual love, and joy. Making love honored them both.

I named the temple in honor of Hathor and Sekhmet. Through the Fellowship of Isis the space was conferred the official status of Iseum, meaning sanctuary or temple.

During the days that Clooney couldn't visit I spent decorating my miniature Temple. All ancient Egyptian temples had the stars of the Duat painted on the ceilings along with Nuit spread across the sky. I found silky, dark blue cloth which I attached to the ceiling of the living room, now a temple. I pasted large gold stars on it. Then found a spectacularly colorful, painted papyrus of Nuit, measuring four feet by ten feet, and fastened it to the ceiling.

I found a wide expanse of gold cloth, then painted hieroglyphics in red paint which translated into "Iseum of Sekhmet and Hathor." The enormous banner covered an entire wall.

A friend who had been to Egypt many times had hundreds of slides of the interior of Seti's Temple at Abydos. I borrowed sixteen of the most vivid slides of Abydos carvings and had them blown up into poster size, then mounted them on the walls. This was before the days of digital cameras.

Afterwards when Saul came to visit me, which he often did, he exclaimed, "Now this feels like a temple."

I researched details involved in consecrating an ancient Egyptian temple. I planned an official consecration, as authentic as I could dream up for that small space. I asked my teacher if he would play Master of Ceremonies for the ritual. I invited my fellow ordained students to practice, along with new priestess and priest friends I had met. I got four bricks and painted them gold, to be the demarcation of the corners of the sacred enclosure. I wrote the litany, using authentic words and actions. Following recipes I found on the internet, I cooked my own natron as well as kyphi incense to use in the ceremony.

Clooney and his wife Valerie attended Egyptian classes with me. The seminar room was not far from their home. Thus they each played speaking roles in the consecration, while Saul watched from the audience. A word that comes to mind for our complicated and entangled relationship is "karmic."

Chapter Fourteen

ONCE THE CREATION of the temple and its consecration was finalized, I looked forward to Clooney spending as much time with me as possible. In the quiet of my room I hungered for him more than ever. Although he visited often, it was never enough. Even after numerous days and nights with him, my craving was prodigious. I wanted him to permanently move in with me.

My life with Saul had been left behind, along with most of my possessions; my intention was that Clooney and I would eventually live together in that tiny apartment. Clooney's ongoing behavior demonstrated that he wanted the same thing.

I discussed the idea of his living with me. Then he explained that he wasn't at liberty to do so. The problem wasn't that he was married. He had an obligation.

He and Valerie had moved into her mother's house to care for the old woman. His mother-in-law was elderly, sick, and showing signs of dementia.

"I promised Valerie that I would be supportive of her and assist until her mother dies, whenever that might be. So living with you is out of the question."

His calm, rational explanation met with hysterics from me. Eventually, though, I grew to accept that limitation.

While a permanent living situation wasn't possible, our connection grew to intense proportions. We were highly telepathic and sensitive to each other. I knew when he was thinking of me. He could do the same. I could feel him many miles away and intuited his emotional condition at any given moment. He knew what I was feeling and thinking often before I did, often from long distances. Plus whenever we heard each other's voice on the phone, we'd experience a sense of "coming home" as well as sexual desire beyond anything either of us had ever experienced before. Our mysterious, penetrating bond had no earthly explanation.

I found that being in relationship with Clooney released all my sexual inhibitions. He emboldened and encouraged my behavior. The energy between us inspired me to be more outrageously sexual and daring. Wild.

Although not proud of my behavior, during this period I had a "one-afternoon" stand with a man I knew. Clooney drove me to the man's house. Presumably the man and I would create a life-sized statue using me as a model. After dropping me off, Clooney left, declaring he would return in an hour or so. I swear that he knew what was going to transpire and went for a drive in order to give space to let it happen.

The man and I had sex.

Afterwards Clooney returned, even helped with the statue, although sexual tension was palpable during the modeling session. Afterwards he drove me back to my place. Neither Clooney nor I discussed what went on that afternoon.

Years earlier, when I was fifteen, I remembered a past life in an Egyptian temple. A notion persisted that I had somehow been "naughty" and had been thrown off a cliff in some sort of ritual. On my first trip to Egypt I found the place where I died—the cliff behind

Hetshepsut's temple. While my tour group explored the temple, sight-seeing, I performed forgiveness work.

After my move to the apartment and our increasing connection, Clooney and I collectively remembered a past life we shared in ancient Egypt, one in which we were involved in a potent, yet destructive relationship with each other.

The memories included Clooney being a High Priest of Kom-Ombo Temple, while I was a humble initiate at Dendera Temple. We recalled with anxiety that Clooney had masterminded my death in that life. On the other hand, I had incited my own demise with jealous and vengeful behavior towards him.

Months before, while I was still living with Saul, I had arranged a tour to Egypt. I'd be returning to Egypt a third time on this tour. An Egyptian friend of mine owned the tour group I'd be using, while eight people had signed up for the tour. Clooney wanted to go with me, especially now that we both had memories of that life together. Saul and Valerie also planned to join the group.

I arranged for an additional week at a timeshare in Aswan, scheduled before the tour began in Cairo. All these plans had been finalized before moving into my apartment and my escalating relationship with Clooney. Once I moved out, Saul and Valerie decided not to join us. That left Clooney and I traveling together. Clooney and Egypt, my two dearest loves. To say I was exhilarated was an understatement.

Prior to leaving on our trip, I had a potent dream, one I've never forgotten. I dreamt that Clooney and I were two serpents, which wound around each other, and then merged into one. The image of a caduceus came to mind, as well as the representation of an awakening kundalini.

Weeks before our tour, Clooney astonished me by announcing he had changed his mind. "I want to move in with you."

He advised me that he only had social security to live on. The house he and Valerie lived in, the furnishings, most of the possessions, and bank accounts belonged to Valerie's mother. In short, he was poor. He had health issues requiring expensive medication in the days before Medicare programs covered prescription drugs. Therefore, his entire income would be required to pay for medicine.

I had a meager income, living on social security along with a small inheritance from my parents. I was an inept business person and my store made little money. Yet I was able to pay my bills. I was financially independent for the first time in my adult life and hated to give it up.

Bluntly I informed Clooney "I don't want to support you." In truth, I didn't have enough money to do so even if I wanted to.

"I don't want to live alone," he declared. "I lived by myself for many years, and I don't want to go through that again."

We were at an impasse. Egypt, and our complicated karma, intertwined like my dream of the two snakes.

Chapter Fifteen

CLOONEY AND I FLEW TO CAIRO. We stayed at a hotel near the airport, heavily protected by machine-gun toting guards. The next day we flew by EgyptAir to Aswan. We took a cab, then a small boat to our temporary home, the Pyramisa Isis Island Resort. My friend and tour guide, along with his wife, met us there.

I was impatient to show Clooney around Egypt, as though I had discovered the ancient world myself. We made plans to visit Philae, Temple of Isis, soon.

Eager to shop for items to sell in my store, Clooney and I took the small boat to Aswan. We wandered the souq near the quay to the Nile cruise ships.

Inside the bazaar stood a galabaya shop. Ramadan was the proud owner of the tiny establishment. His store was crammed, wall to wall, floor to ceiling, with stunning, affordable galabayas. Ramadan's galabayas were traditional Egyptian garments made from fine Egyptian cotton. They were floor-length, many with long sleeves. Others had short cuffed sleeves. Most of the galabayas were intricately embroidered. I had stepped into galabaya heaven.

Ramadan usually spent his days in a little niche in the corner of his shop, watching popular Egyptian soap operas on his small screen TV, brewing pots of mint tea, while endlessly smoking American cigarettes. His brother ran the shop and conducted business with the customers, unless a problem arose for Ramadan to handle.

I was conscious of the protocol for women's dress in that Muslim country. I had purchased galabayas on my first two trips and was wearing my favorite, a short-sleeved, turquoise blue, embroidered, floor-length galabaya. I also wore anklets with tiny bells on them. The anklets tinkled when I walked.

I was engrossed with the magnificent galabayas hung everywhere, and didn't notice Ramadan emerging from his grotto, staring at me. Suddenly I felt his presence and turned.

He was dressed in a gleaming white galabaya with a black abaya over it; a sleeveless, floor-length vest. Although Ramadan was only forty, he looked at least twenty years older. Balding, care-worn, sad. Our eyes met. He wasn't a stranger. I knew him, but not from this life.

"I heard you come in," he explained in perfect English. I found out later that Ramadan spoke many languages, learned from years of selling to foreigners. He smiled and his dark, attractive face lit up. He, like other Nubians living in Aswan, was quite handsome.

I grinned in reply. "My anklets."

"Yes," he continued. "I never talk to customers any more. That's my brother's job." His face wrinkled in puzzlement. "Do I know you? Have I met you before? I must be acquainted with you."

"No," I replied. "Yet you are familiar to me, too."

After showing me many galabayas, I purchased a dozen. Eventually I would buy more than thirty to take home for resale in my own store.

Ramadan invited Clooney and me into his private space, inviting us to sit. He offered us mint tea. Ramadan and I smoked cigarettes. Clooney smoked a pipe. The three of us puffed away. Drank endless cups of tea. Talked. Becoming better acquainted. Laughing like old friends.

During the week we stayed at the resort, Clooney and I enjoyed the breakfast buffet at the Pyramisa. Then we traveled the short journey by boat to the Aswan bazaar, and to Ramadan's shop. He greeted us every morning like long-lost family. We smoked. Drank mint tea. With every passing day, Ramadan face grew younger and younger. Until finally, he looked his age. He seemed happier as well.

He told us stories of how he started working when he was nine years old, common in that impoverished country. He worked hard from dawn until midnight. Then he borrowed money from the government bank in order to start his own shop. He supported himself, his wife, and three children, one of whom was attending university. The other two would go to college when they were of age. Ramadan also provided for his brother, his sister-in-law and their two children.

He explained he and his wife had married when quite young. Their marriage had been arranged by their families. They didn't meet until the wedding. Although he had three children, Ramada told me he had never been in love. Nor did he have time for love, laboring seven days a week just to make a living.

Sometimes Clooney got restless after we talked awhile and he wandered the Oriental-style market. He met another shop owner two doors down and they became friends, talking for hours. Therefore, I was often alone with Ramadan in his cubbyhole.

Ramadan's flirting was shy and tentative at first. Over the hours and days we spent together, aided by my friendliness, he became playful, then romantic.

I admit I was foolhardy. What was the matter with me? As though I was drunk on romance and sexuality. How could I act this way with a man I hardly knew, a foreign man at that, with Clooney in my life? I was deeply in love with Clooney yet…I continued to act out a personal drama that made no sense.

While holding my hand in his private alcove, so that no Muslim eyes could observe us, Ramadan proclaimed, "I've fallen in love with you. I want to marry you and take care of you," he told me. "By Muslim law I am allowed to have four wives, so long as I can provide for each one. I only have one. I make enough money to get you an apartment and take care of you for the rest of your life."

"I'm flattered," I told him. "I like you a lot, too. However, I would drive you crazy in no time. I'm a very stubborn, independent American woman. Strong willed. Not really good wife material. And I'm not Muslim."

Tears trickled down his handsome black cheeks. "But I love you," he repeated.

"I know, honey. But it's not possible. In time you would be miserable with me.

His eyes disagreed with me. He lit up another cigarette and sipped his tea, reflecting quietly.

I didn't know what else to say. Later on I found out this was a common practice with Egyptian men and Western women. The state would officially marry them. The woman would spend a few weeks or a month with the Egyptian man. He provided a nice home and furnishings, bought presents for her. They would meet once a year. Then the woman would return home. A short romantic, sexual intermezzo for both, sanctioned by the state and the religion. I later met couples who had continued their official marriage/affair for years or even decades.

The last day Clooney and I spent in Aswan, Ramadan decided to rent a felluca with a man to navigate it. He invited Clooney and I to join him. As we walked down the avenue to the boat dock, Ramadan walked far ahead of us. We were not allowed to walk on the street with him. Clooney, because he was a Westerner, and me because I was a woman as well as a foreigner. Married Egyptian couples were forbidden, under penalty of torture and imprisonment, to walk together, hold hands, kiss, or show any affection.

As we strolled behind him, I reflected on living in Egypt with Ramadan. I felt comfortable and friendly with him. I loved Egypt as I had loved no other place on earth. I was strangely at home in Egypt. I would adore living there.

But…Egypt was unbearably hot most of the year. It was dirty; full of viruses and bacteria, a third-world country, impoverished in the extreme. Egypt was predominately Muslim, which I saw as punitive towards women. Women were property, as they had been in earlier centuries, and men could treat them as they saw fit. It was also a difficult country to get around, lacking any decent transportation. Almost no one except hotel and shop owners spoke English. And it was a dictatorship, with harsh rules and arbitrary punishment. So, did I want to live in Egypt? No. Not to mention, I was in deeply love with Clooney.

We got to the dock and silently stepped into the boat. A man navigated it to a small, almost-deserted island downriver from Aswan. During the journey the three of us sat self-consciously on the seats, pretending not to even be acquainted with each other. Feigning lack of interest. Not even talking.

When we pulled up to a sandy beach, we wordlessly climbed out. Ramadan led the way to a part of the beach that couldn't be seen from the river. He pulled off his abaya and spread it on the ground, motioning me to lay down.

I did so, almost as if I were in a dream. Ramadan pulled up my galabaya and proceeded to make love to me. Clooney kissed me the entire time. It was the most erotic, exciting experience of my life. Then the three of us composed ourselves, returned to the boat, and motored back to Aswan, expressionless and quiet once again.

We had been invited to dinner at Ramadan's house that evening. He drove us there in his old silver Mercedes, a status symbol. His wife and daughters had prepared a feast for us. I found the evening at his home, the lavish meal, and meeting his family, surreal, confusing, and disconcerting.

Clooney and I then took the shuttle back to our hotel. We never spoke of the occurrence until fifteen years later. He claimed not to remember that afternoon.

The next day was our last in Aswan. Our tour was scheduled to meet in Cairo in two days, then immediately go by van to Mena House Hotel in Giza, overlooking the pyramids. Clooney went to say goodbye to his friend in the other shop in the bazaar. I went to Ramadan's galabaya shop. He took me into a private alley to say goodbye. He kissed me. And cried. Made me promise to meet him in Greece the following summer, where we could be together without prying eyes.

I called Ramadan from California as often as I could afford, but quickly lost touch. With Egypt being isolated, without modern conveniences, and before the explosion of cellphones, losing track was the norm rather than the exception.

In 2000 Egypt, because of its faltering economy, called in government loans, like the one Ramadan took out to expand his shop. During my last phone call to Ramadan, he told me he had been one of 10,000 people who went to prison for months because he couldn't repay the loan. He was released after his family sold everything in order to liberate him. That was before the Arab Spring. I often wonder what happened to Ramadan. Is he even alive?

As I look back after so much time has elapsed, I remember these details distinctly. I'm not proud of myself.

What was my affair with Ramadan about? Why did I act the way I did? Why did Clooney leave Ramadan and me alone, allowing space for feelings to ripen? Why didn't he say anything to me at the time? Why doesn't he remember the incident on the beach? How could I experience being with another man while being in love with Clooney?

Mysterious.

Were our karmic influences playing out? Not just once, but over and over. Countless revolutions round an intricate maze of connections. A curious and often painful karmic circuit.

Chapter Sixteen

CLOONEY AND I LEFT ASWAN to meet up with our tour group in Giza, at the Mena House Hotel. We were so focused on details that we didn't talk about what had transpired in Aswan.

Our tiny group of eight people plus Clooney and me settled in. Our tour began. While in Giza I fell ill and had to rest in bed. Clooney took over the day-to-day running of the tour arrangements. He had been involved in the travel industry many years before and was able and willing.

Once I joined the group again, I found he had become chummy with a woman of the group. Whether or not he was romantically interested, I don't know. He tells me he wasn't. But I found his rapport interesting in light of Ramadan.

Was he seeking revenge? Was he letting me know he also was independent? That he was free to do what he wanted? Maybe we were both exceptionally susceptible to the opposite sex, even though we loved each other. Or were we absurdly unable to be monogamous with each other?

Clooney and I were both adult children of alcoholics. We each experienced sexual abuse and molestation at the hands of our opposite sex parent. Therefore, we are deeply wounded individuals, especially regarding sex. Perhaps that is the only logical explanation.

During the next ten days, Clooney kept me at arm's length, while he grew closer to the woman. Although never a communicator of his feelings, now he said almost nothing. He was moody and grim except around his new woman friend.

While we had been in Aswan, Clooney and I made plans to have a spiritual wedding ritual at the temple of Dendera. We had purchased two spectacular galabayas from Ramadan. Clooney ordered matching gold rings for our ceremony in the shape of snakes with ruby eyes, based on the dream I had back home before our trip.

I wrote a special litany for the ritual and each member of our tour group had agreed to play a speaking role.

But when the time came Clooney didn't put on his galabaya. He clowned his way through the ritual, then left suddenly to smoke his pipe and sit in the tour bus. I was stunned and bewildered.

When we got to our hotel that night, I asked him to tell me what was going on. He was silent. I begged him. Cried. Pleaded. Threatened. Cried some more. No answer was forthcoming.

The next day we flew back to Giza. Still he said nothing. We said our farewells to the tour group and boarded the plane back to the United States. He was quiet all through the long flight home.

But inwardly I seethed. Finally my anger burst out. "If this is the way you're going to treat me, I wouldn't want to live with you."

Still no response. He stared out the plane's window at clouds. Only the sky knew what was on his mind.

His wife Valerie picked him up at the airport. Saul was on hand at baggage claim to drive me back to my apartment.

Clooney gave me a perfunctory hug and was gone. That was April 1. April Fool's Day. I knew that he was leaving me. Had left me. But why? Was it Ramadan?

Valerie apparently told Saul, while Clooney and I were in Egypt that if he, Clooney, didn't break up with me, she was divorcing him. Had Valerie given him an ultimatum? Was that why his behavior was strange?

Clooney had promised to help me set up my Egyptian merchandise at a fair. He kept his word. Yet he never spoke of anything except mundane details.

He returned the items and me to my apartment, then sat down on the futon. Silent. Brooding.

I asked him what was going on. No response. No matter what I did or said, he said nothing in return.

Finally he announced, "I'm leaving," and went to the front door.

Dramatically I flung myself in front of it and said, "You're not leaving here until you explain to me what's happening." Then I added, "Sekhmet is on my side."

He scowled. "You forget. Sekhmet is on my side too."

"True." I looked him in the eyes. "What are you so afraid of?" I asked him quietly.

He broke down and cried. He returned to the futon and wept for an hour.

I put my arms around him, comforting him. "Tell me," I beseeched him. "Tell me what is going on. I can stand anything so long as I know what it is."

He continued to cry wordlessly. Then he said in a muffled voice, "I'm such a coward."

"What does that mean?" I asked him. "What are you a coward about?"

No response. He got up to leave.

I watched him go out the front door, shutting it silently behind him. I didn't stop him this time.

I wrote letters to him. They came back addressed "Return to sender."

I sent emails. No response. Not a word.

I left numerous phone calls. No response.

I continued to run my store, and sold merchandise on the internet and at fairs. Working gave me something to focus on, to turn my attention away from grief. Every time I stopped for even a moment, the tears began.

Heartbreak is a melodramatic, exaggerated word, but I knew what it felt like. My chest ached.

Months went by. A year. No communication from Clooney. No explanation. I attempted to resolve my confusion and sadness without knowing or understanding anything.

My friend Delores invited me to attend a metaphysical conference, a two-day event, in Palm Springs. We arranged to stay in a nearby hotel.

My friend Elaine (yes, the same one) warned me that Clooney and his wife Valerie were also going to be present at the event. Upset at the news, I decided to go anyway.

As I listened to the speakers, one ear was attuned to their arrival. The evening ended but the couple hadn't shown up. As I moved through the crowd and got to the back door, I saw them standing together. I felt joy at seeing them again. I walked up and hugged them both. They acted happy to see me. Then I left quickly. As I got outside I felt the grief start again. Delores caught up with me and we returned to our hotel room.

After Delores went to sleep, I spent the entire night thinking. I wouldn't open up access to my feelings again. It had taken tremendous effort to get the door to my heart closed. I didn't know if I could seal it again.

At a break during the next day's conference, I went outside to smoke a cigarette. Clooney casually strolled over to me, like he had just seen me the day before. As if nothing unusual had transpired between us during the past year.

He spoke tenderly. "I've missed you so much." I could feel the emotional hook, as I was reeled in again by his words.

I blurted out, "You could have fooled me!" It was a cruel thing to say. Yet understandable due to his total lack of communication.

He strolled back into the building and out of my life.

I needed to escape. Delores was tired. So we packed up and left before the conference ended.

I wouldn't see Clooney again for fourteen years.

Chapter Seventeen

I GRIEVED. I YEARNED. I ached for Clooney. He didn't contact me. I didn't contact him.

I operated my business.

Dated a little.

Had more and more contact with Saul. Then I received an intuitive message that Saul and I would be getting back together again. I mentioned it to him.

"Oh, no," he replied firmly. "That will never happen." Famous last words. In fact, Saul was fond of saying, "Never say never."

A year later, sometime after September 11, I lost most of my inheritance. Many people lost money in 2002, during a mini stock market crash. I couldn't afford to live by myself any more.

Saul got sick. He also needed surgery.

We decided to move back in together. Bought a small house with the remains of my legacy and his earnings.

Although my life stabilized, my melancholy did not. Until Saul and I moved to Washington State, I continued to pine for Clooney. Once we moved there and bought a permaculture farm, my thoughts of Clooney grew dimmer, but never disappeared altogether.

Saul and I worked hard. But we weren't farmers. We always needed help. The small farm took a toll on us. Saul's health wasn't good. Furthermore, he wasn't a young man. When we sold our farm and moved to Port Townsend, Saul had turned eighty-seven.

Saul's health deteriorated steadily. His ankle tendons were giving out, making it hard for him to walk. His spine curved alarmingly. He lost three inches in height during the next two years.

Then he had two heart attacks. Stents were implanted. He was put on powerful medications. Because I'm an empath, the poorer his health became, the worse I felt.

In August, Saul was diagnosed with colon cancer. He refused chemotherapy and radiation. Surgery was the best treatment. Most of his colon was removed. The surgery was a success. But his kidneys began to fail. Four days later Saul died of renal failure.

I had been with Saul for a total of twenty-three years. Our relationship wasn't romantically obsessive as with Clooney, but I loved Saul dearly. Best of all we were friends. I missed him.

Two months later I received another intuitive message. "Find Clooney on the internet. Send him a letter."

Fearful, yet hopeful, I located him, then sent him a letter about Saul's passing. The two men had, after all, been friends.

A month lapsed with no reply. How foolish of me to believe that interactions between Clooney and me could be any different than previously.

On Thanksgiving, I spent time with several friends. I was despondent. "I'm lonely. I want a love relationship."

They were supportive and kind.

The evening after Thanksgiving I was sitting at my computer, playing Scrabble.

A call came through in the middle of my game. Hastily the caller hung up. Phone numbers automatically show up on my laptop screen.

The screen showed the phone number. I didn't know anyone in the displayed area code. It was too late in the evening for sales calls. Curious, I called the number.

"Hi. Did you just call me?"

A very familiar voice answered, "Uh huh."

"Clooney? Clooney?? Clooney!!" I exclaimed, not believing it could be him. It had been fourteen years since I had heard his voice or had any communication with him.

He explained, "I was entering your phone number on my new smart phone and it called you accidentally. I hung up before it rang."

We had a shy conversation at first, but gained confidence the longer we talked.

After almost an hour, as we were getting ready to say goodbye, I blurted out, "I've never stopped loving you." I surprised myself. Because I was dazed, I can't remember what he said after that. Maybe he said I love you too. I don't recollect. We hung up.

The next night we talked again for more than an hour at a more meaningful, personal level than the night before.

I found out he was still living with his wife Valerie. I reminded him that he would have to tell her we were talking again. I hate secrecy. Not only that, but I believe everyone is psychic on some level, particularly wives. So Valerie would know.

"I'll tell her when the time is right," he promised.

The third night in a row we chatted again, this time around 1 AM. He was talking from his office. I was in mine.

Early in our conversation Clooney announced, "I'm moving in with you."

"You are!?" I was dumbfounded. "It's a miracle we're back together. I feel the same towards you as I always have. I love you dearly."

He agreed. "I've loved you for years…and years…and years. It is a miracle."

"The universe does some pretty amazing things."

"I've been debating with myself for over a month, thinking about calling you. I read and reread your letter dozens of times." He well understood the problems calling me would mean in his life. "We won't have much money. But we'll be together," he said.

"I don't care about money," I replied. "Just to be with you is enough. I've been waiting so long. I never thought we would get together again. You can move into my house with me."

We crooned for a while as lovers do, formulating plans.

"I want to come up to Port Townsend and visit you very soon," he told me. "I don't want to wait. Then I'll come back here and pack."

"When?"

"Before Christmas."

"Christmas is only a few weeks away."

Just then Clooney murmured, "Valerie is standing in the doorway, listening, with a weird expression on her face, shaking her head."

"She knows," I told him. "Go talk to her now. You don't get to wait for the proper time. The time is now."

He hesitated.

"I'll be here, loving you," I told him. "Just tell her the truth. You don't have to be guilty for having feelings."

"Talk to you later," and he hung up.

I could intuit him the rest of the night and couldn't sleep because of his distress. It wasn't the first time our telepathy was undeniable. He was fearful. Terribly stressed. I prayed that he be protected and comforted.

Chapter Eighteen

I DIDN'T HEAR FROM Clooney for a couple of days. I "held" him protectively in my thoughts, imagining what enormous stress he was under.

When he finally called me, he related, "I told Valerie I'm leaving her."

Mind boggling. He had never told her that before. Nor had he ever made that kind of well-defined resolution regarding me. I had waited twenty-five years to hear those words. All I could do was thank him, and the universe, for the great gift bestowed on me. Before he went to sleep he sent me an electronic communication: "Love you. Love you. Love you. Me."

We talked intermittently. Yet I could feel him with me every day, a physical presence that was powerfully, overwhelmingly, telepathically loving and sexual.

"I still have the ring and the scarf you gave me years ago," I texted him. "I have a king sized bed, now, too." Beds had been a standing joke between us because of the too-small bed in my former apartment fourteen years before. We had often rolled off that bed while making love.

He sent a sizzling reply. "What a visual. A ring. A scarf. A king sized bed. And you. And me. Wow!"

I sighed with rapture when I received his message. I was burning up. I couldn't contain myself and sent him a passionate vow. "I relinquish myself to you. I'm yours. I pledge myself to you as your soul mate, your twin soul, playmate, lover, life companion, fellow adventurer, psychic, priestess, friend—and your beloved."

The night before he set off on his long trek from California to Washington, he sent me a text message: "Good nite my twin. I am all packed and ready to go. Much to talk about. I am ecstatic…Talk once I am on the road…I am in bliss. Love you, Me." And then as an afterthought a second text: "Twin as in twin soul my darling soul mate. XXXXXOO."

Clooney had never been an emotionally articulate man, keeping his thoughts and feelings well hidden. Therefore, his words transported me onto a sea of elation, where I bobbed like a buoy in the gentle swells of his affection.

His trip from southern California to northern Washington I consider a Hero's Journey. He experienced a grueling three days in his pickup truck. First Clooney sloshed through a huge rain storm. Further north he was stranded in a blizzard. Drove at a snail's pace over countless miles of freeway construction. The last day he decided to push on through until he was at my side. He arrived in Port Townsend at five in the morning, exhausted and bleary-eyed, having been helplessly lost in unlit, narrow back roads all night.

During the last eight hours, we had kept continuously connected via our cell phones. He had his phone on the seat next to him, my voice keeping him company through the seemingly-endless trek.

Once he got to town, he was on the verge of collapse. "I can't go any further. I'm in a parking lot of a store. It's all lit up, with Santa and reindeers on the roof." His voice was incoherent with exhaustion.

I knew where he was. "Stay where you are," I told him. "I'll come get you." I changed into jeans and a jacket and frantically drove the ten minutes to the edge of town. He sounded terrible. I worried that perhaps he had suffered a stroke or was having a blood sugar problem.

I saw the running lights of his truck as I neared the store. Feverishly, I pulled into the lot, then jumped out of my vehicle and ran over to him.

The man I saw stumble out of the driver's door was nothing like the man I had last seen fourteen years ago. He had visibly aged into a skinny, wobbly old man. From a distance and in the dark, he looked like he was near death's door.

For months I had wondered what a man of eighty-two would look like. I had scrutinized men I saw in the grocery store, trying to imagine how Clooney would appear after fourteen years. I was not prepared for the man he had become. I threw myself into his arms anyway and hugged him fiercely to me.

With effort he pushed me away. "There's time for that later. First take me to your house."

"Of course." I drove to my home, overwhelmed by the enormous changes in him, while he slowly followed me in his huge truck.

Once we were safe in the warmth and radiance of my home, he perked up and we kissed intensely. Then I led him down the hallway to my room. Took off our clothes. Laid down in my king size bed, kissing frenziedly.

He positioned himself between my legs and moved up and down. "I love our bodies," he declared.

Nausea rose up in me, unwanted, unsolicited.

The man I used to love wasn't with me. In his place was a strange old man.

He had lost thirty-eight pounds, dropping from a sturdy 196 to 158. He used to be five feet, eleven inches tall, but in the interim had lost three inches in height. His skinny ribs poked me painfully as he moved against me. His chest was misshapen and scarred from several surgeries. Then I noticed his fingers, hands, and lower arms. They were blackened from the side effects of various medications he had been taking. His beautiful, thick silver hair had thinned to cotton candy tufts. Many teeth were missing. His ankles and feet were tinged an unnatural purple hue from neuropathy. His right foot had a partially amputated toe, while sores seeped and bled from the sole.

Unable to control my heartache, and incapable of making love to him any further, I kissed his stained hands and fingers. "Your poor hands," I murmured tenderly, tears gushing.

"What is it, sweetie?" he asked me, bewildered by my sudden emotion. The voice and accent was familiar, even his energy, but not the physical body.

I closely my eyes remembering him as he used to be. I blubbered, "You've changed so much."

"I'm still the same man inside," he replied soothingly.

Then I cried so intensely that all he could do was gather me into his scrawny, discolored arms. He held me gently until my extreme reaction subsided.

When I had calmed down, he kissed me. Then maneuvered on top and began to make love to me again. Suddenly I was overwhelmed and horrified with shame. An old, unfamiliar man was being intimate with me while I watched, detaching myself, disembodied. As though I was four years old and my Uncle Dodie was molesting me again.

He passed out while making love to me, as if he was sinking into a coma. I crawled out from under him, rolled away, and carefully got out of bed. Covered him with the comforter, closed the door softly, and tiptoed to the guest bedroom, not wanting to wake him. He was drained from the long, arduous drive. His energy had been consumed from his hero's journey to reunite with me.

Shivering I got into the tiny twin bed, trying to find comfort and warmth. My feet and ankles burned painfully and relentlessly. I don't have any physical problems, so I must have been empathically feeling his diabetic neuropathy. Repulsion and shame screamed throughout my consciousness. Grief for the loss of the man I had once loved. Confusion rolling over me like hammering surf. Sorrow for an unrequited dream that had evaporated beneath the twinkling lights of Santa and his reindeer.

Chapter Nineteen

RESTLESS AND AGITATED, I crawled out of bed, got dressed and went to my office. Poured out my sad story onto my laptop. I couldn't stand Clooney to be in my house one minute longer. I prayed fervently, "Please don't let him die in my bed!"

Hours later Clooney woke up and came to find me.

I went to his side and impulsively knelt in front of him, blurting out "I need for you to leave. Today." I glanced up at his stricken face. "Please forgive me. Please forgive me. Please forgive me!" I wailed.

I made breakfast while he dressed.

He was quiet and thoughtful, but his eyes appeared alternately angry, sad and confused. I didn't blame him.

"Why?" he finally asked.

"I don't know," I replied quietly.

"You know, this is a bad thing you're doing."

I remained defenseless. "I realize that."

"I should have known you'd leave me again."

I looked pleadingly into his eyes. I had no response. "I have no defense."

He changed his tactic. "We could have stayed friends. But not now. I can't trust you."

"I understand." I sighed.

Then like a slippery karmic serpent, our connection grabbed hold of me. I felt it deeply inside. It drew me to him. He came over and kissed me. I could always feel his power overriding my will. This was no exception.

I resisted mightily. I didn't want to be ensnared, not with mixed emotions. With difficulty I broke our embrace. "I'll drive you to a local hotel. You can rest up before you drive back."

He followed me in his massive truck. I drove past the entryway of the hotel facing the Puget Sound. He pulled in and parked near the lobby. I continued driving through the parking lot, not stopping, heading frantically towards home. I glanced at him. He was standing outside the driver's door now, staring at me. That image of him would haunt me.

As soon as I returned home, I mourned. For days. Going over and over the memories. The years we had known each other. Our love-making in all its different locales and guises. The recent past when we had talked lovingly on the phone. We had been excited like two children waiting for a desired toy. Sexual passion running through us like an uninsulated electric wire. Now he was gone again.

This time I had sent him away. I had no choice.

I wrote him endless texts and emails. "I know you can never forgive me. But please forgive me." Many days and nights I could sense him telepathically. Feel him making love to me, holding me, communing with me.

Then I decided to explain my experience that awful day at my house.

"Dearest Clooney—I believe I've had contact with you many times in the last few weeks, since your hero's journey to Port Townsend and back to California. I feel pain sometimes. Often I think I hear your voice or feel your despair. One night the burning pain, tingling, and numbness in my feet, ankles and hands was unbearable for hours. I don't have diabetes, so I'm assuming it was your pain. I've grieved, especially re-reading our text messages to each other, but other times, too. This morning early I felt you again and we "talked."

"I know it's sad that our love affair is over. Maybe we're not destined to be together in this life. I surrender to a higher power, karma, destiny, or whatever that makes it so. I've contemplated many times about the day you arrived here at my home and there's nothing different I could have done. I feel sorry for how I've hurt you. I didn't intend to hurt you. Up until you arrived, I thought everything was fine and I was in bliss waiting for you, thinking our protracted wait was over.

"Our connection lives on between our souls. I love you and always will love you. I have loved you since that first day when you met me and our joy came to life together.

"I don't see any reason for me to slink off without another word to you. That isn't my way or who I am. Perhaps my words reopen your wounds or confuse you. I hope not. I hope my words are comforting, a balm. I have your back. I sit beside you on your continuing journey, through dark and rain and blizzard, my voice soothing in your ear, like the cell phone in your truck.

"I wasn't lonely and missing Saul. I was joyful. I still am filled with joy and enjoying life. I got a message from my Elders to write to you, and was hesitant, but took a chance. I'm taking another chance now, not because I'm lonely but because of the connection that I feel with you that I openly acknowledge.

"We're not lovers. We may not be friends. Maybe we're much more than friends. I have no word for it. Could it be that we really are soul twins?

"If you want to ignore me and this message, I accept that. If you're angry and can't trust me, there's nothing I can say to that. If you want to email me or call me, I welcome it. This is about a miraculous connection, something mysterious and wonderful and divine that doesn't come to two people very often. Something to celebrate.

"That all I have to say for now. Have a happy holiday, my dear one. Love, Lauren"

He continued to visit me telepathically. Although I received no reply, I contacted him again a few weeks later.

"Dear Clooney—I can imagine that you are angry at me or hurt or both, not to mention confused. You told me you could never trust me again. I can understand why you would believe that.

"Yet over the last few days (and other days since you were here in Port Townsend) I have felt you with me strongly, exactly the way I did during our short reunion by phone and text, and other times in our long history. The feelings I get are unmistakable, and wildly physical. I only feel those when you are thinking about me, and perhaps thinking about me in an intimate way. And particularly last night. You visited me energetically and we made love.

"So I am emboldened to contact you again. So far you haven't told me to stop contacting you, only no response.

"I believe we are still deeply, cosmically connected. I love you profoundly and miss you, miss your voice, your love. I believe you still love me, too.

"I can imagine the interaction we had, and the things I told you and asked for, when you were here, made no sense to you. I remember it clearly, vividly, physically, mentally, emotionally. For me there was nothing else I could have done. I would choose my decision again today as I had literally no choice. What I felt and what I had to do was horrifically upsetting, since I was looking forward to us being together at last and my heart—which had been in ecstasy and bliss—broke. When we were together and all hell broke loose for me, reality shattered my/our dreams. Although I experienced it, I can't tell you why it was. I can only describe it.

"Because of that maybe we are not supposed to live together, travel together, or to be together in any kind of close proximity in any way. The intense and profound feelings I experienced were: burning of my skin and insides; intense and deep shame; needing to physically remove myself (since this is my house I needed for you to go away), to the point I couldn't even sleep in the same bed with you nor could I tolerate your presence.

"Nor could I sleep in another bed even though I was exhausted, while my mind and emotions felt strangely tortured. (I'm glad you slept a bit.) In addition my hands, feet, and ankles burned and tingled horribly and unrelentingly as though they were in a cauldron of boiling hot liquid— perhaps picking up your physical sensations of diabetic neuropathy.

"What I propose is that we acknowledge our connection which doesn't die, and attempt to communicate by phone, text, email. I want for you to feel loved and nurtured, held safe in my emotional arms, as I did for you during that awful trip. I want to feel our love as I know it exists. I yearn to hear your voice again and to laugh with you.

"You will stay with Valerie, not having to move any of your belongings, nor disrupt your life in any way. You'll still have your home, books, library, computer, doctors, friends, children, financial stability, all without guilt. I know I couldn't care for your illness as Valerie has done and as she will continue to do. And my darling, you are quite ill. I don't know how you made the trip up here and back again. I shudder to think of it.

"I'm acutely sensitive, empathic, a conduit. I pick up others' physical problems and symptoms (psychically) in my own body, especially if I live with someone. As Saul got sicker, so did I. When he took his medications, I felt the side effects. I thought I was going to die several times, but instead he had heart attacks, then cancer, and he died.

"My friend Susie died in November of congestive heart failure. Whenever I talked with her I'd get breathing problems and heart palpitations. All that stopped immediately when she died. And the other sensations stopped when Saul died as well.

"So I can see that living with someone is very problematic for me. And to live with someone who is as ill as you are would be difficult and painful for me and you would experience the fallout of my difficulties. Perhaps that's why I had the extreme reactions I did when you arrived here. Perhaps it was my higher self, protecting me, protecting us, maybe even Valerie.

"I think we were both living in a lovely dream, of what might have been. Now we can face the reality of what is, including our limitations.

"What do you think? Feel? Would you be willing to attempt real communication with me? Since you and I wouldn't be lovers anymore, Valerie wouldn't have to be afraid or angry and you could relax. Call me my darling. With all my heart."

I desired fervently for him to call but tried not to hope. Hope is a fantasy. To live in hope kills the soul.

Late at night, I could feel his psychic power and body heat. He traveled across space and time to make love to me again. After we had cuddled for a while, despite my good intentions, I sent him a text.

"You're thinking strongly of me. I can tell. Wanna talk?"

The next day I traveled from Port Townsend across Puget Sound to Whidbey Island. The house that had been bequeathed to me from Saul was in jeopardy. Once in Coupeville at my lawyer's office, I was given bad news. The title to the deed might have to go into probate, which would be very costly. I could even lose the house to Saul's children. Afterwards, while waiting in line for the ferry to return home, I was distraught and terrified.

Just then I picked up a psychic message from beyond. "Don't worry. You will be taken care of."

In the next moment my cell phone buzzed with a text message. The juxtaposition of mere seconds between the two messages was extraordinary.

It was from Clooney. "Sweetheart. Thinking strongly of you....xxxx me."

Chapter Twenty

I TEXTED HIM BACK. "Oh Clooney. Clooney. I weep with joy as I read your message.—Love."

Later that day I received his short but poignant message. "I xxxx you."

Thus began yet another episode in our enigmatic and tangled relationship. He had forgiven me and still loved me.

For me, nothing had changed. I adored him the same as I always had. I was enthralled by him. By our connection. The telepathic, intensely physical and sensual bond, and love, was still unbroken.

Yet I had to shift my perspective in order to think about him in his altered body. Whenever I thought about him, sent messages, or conversed with Clooney, I forced myself to remember the older physical body he currently inhabited.

Such is the reality of aging. Loving someone who used to be younger but now is elderly. Fifteen years had elapsed without watching the changes manifest, day by day, year by year. I was trying to recover from the cruel shock, from memory into reality.

Inexplicably I was still madly in love with him. Couldn't bear to be apart from him. Sent him endless texts and emails. Phoned at least daily.

"Please let me fly down to California and spend time with you," I begged. "That way you don't have to exhaust yourself with driving. This time it will be the heroine's Journey."

He agreed. "We can see how we do together."

Yet we couldn't decide on a date.

Meantime I continued to flood him with words—on his cellphone, text, emails. I couldn't say enough. Words linked me to him. He didn't reply much, while I couldn't stop communicating.

For every message Clooney sent, I sent twenty. Yet what precious messages I did receive, I memorized every syllable, intonation, and nuance. Immersing myself through eyes and ears.

"I guess there's no reason to postpone our meeting any longer," he announced on February 24th, surprising me as always. "How about February 28? Fly down to Bakersfield. Stay for five days or so?"

"Okay!" Immediately I went on the internet and bought my ticket to happiness, and began counting the hours. I wondered how I would react this time. I had been practicing new memories of him, the way he was now, after fifteen years.

During our last phone call the night before I left, I teased him that I was looking forward to a hot bath with him.

I took a shuttle to the airport, fairly humming with enthusiasm. My personality had changed over the last few months, becoming energetically extroverted and friendly. Was this due to Saul's passing away? Or because I had re-started a love relationship with Clooney? Or both?

Once having arrived at SeaTac, a series of delays began, which continued at San Francisco International. The journey was similar to Clooney's trip to Washington, but now in reverse. For frustrating hours, we stayed in touch by cellphone. If my excitement had wings, I could have flown to his side without an airplane.

He had already checked into our hotel, and was keeping track of the delays from the concierge desk. Sending me periodic updates on text message. His voice emanating from the small piece of electronic plastic kept me sane.

I was shuttled from one terminal to another, as flights continued to be delayed or cancelled. Transferred to one gate and another. Up and down stairs. In and out of elevators, pulling my carry-on, avoiding further delays from baggage claim.

Late in the evening passengers were informed that the flight crew had gone home and the plane now sat empty on the tarmac. I talked to several young passengers from another flight, who had already waited overnight, almost thirty-six hours, and still no aircraft was available for them. What if the same thing happened to me? Clooney and I only had a few precious days together, and the minutes were inexorably ticking by.

Then good news. I was moved back to the original gate, where I was informed that a fresh crew had come on board. Our plane would be on our way to Bakersfield shortly. The other passengers and I shouted with relief.

The last message from him was informational as well as hilarious. "Fly ops says 5303 departs SFO 6:54. Arrive Bakersfield 8:10 PM. Bath cold. Clooney hottttt.... mmmmm."

The short trip to southern California was uneventful, except for turbulence. Thus our beverage service was cancelled. No matter. In little over an hour I would be with him.

Once the plane had landed and arrived at the gate, I grabbed my suitcase and ran for the waiting area. I could hardly stay inside my skin.

The tiny terminal was empty except for him standing quietly, waiting for me. I swooped over and hugged him tightly. Kissed him. He took my hand and led me outside to the waiting taxi, which in minutes arrived at our hotel. He smiled and greeted the young woman at the hotel desk, then continued to our room. Opened the door for me. Our room was warm, bright, and inviting. A king size bed took up much of the space.

Without hesitation I flung off my clothes and dropped them to the floor. He undressed slowly, folding every piece carefully. Then we moved to the bed.

For the next four days we hardly left that bed. We made love for hours at a time. Slept little. Often after I had been asleep for a while, I woke, sensing his energy. I opened my eyes to see him staring at me with a smoldering look. Then he gathered me into his arms and we continued undiminished. If anything, the intensity and quality of our lovemaking grew the more we re-discovered each other's bodies.

We went out to eat as necessary, then returned to our honeymooning. The words ecstasy, bliss, sensual delirium, sound tame compared to what transpired in that room between us. Nothing in my life ever matched that homecoming.

However, our karmic demon wasn't pacified. Two major quarrels erupted during that short interval. The second row was intense. I had questioned him impulsively, stepping over an important boundary without realizing it.

He glared at me with hostility, closing himself off to me.

I was sure we were breaking up.

"We can still be friends," he muttered, in appeasement, his feline eyes mere slits.

"I don't know if I can be just friends," I replied sorrowfully. "I'm too attached to being lovers."

Teeth clenched, arms folded over his chest, he sat seething, his thoughts far away, as if he had turned to marble.

Helpless in the face of his rage, I could do nothing but sit on the floor next to him, hopeless, in despair.

After a long quiet time, his body relaxed. His hand slithered over to me, seemingly without his volition. I took his hand tentatively. He pulled me to him and kissed me hard. Then flung me onto the bed and sprang on top, intensely making love to me. I melted. Our battle was over. The demon was back in its cage.

When I asked him later what had happened, he told me that he must have been feeling pre-separation stress, but wouldn't explain any further.

We had decided to stay together until late that afternoon, when my plane was due to fly north. I thought he would accompany me to the airport, but he didn't. Instead he called a cab to deliver me.

We had to say our goodbyes on the hotel patio, while the taxi driver waited. Still not fully recovered from our argument, we tentatively kissed. He seemed detached, cool and distant. What would our future hold? Confused, I got in and the driver drove me the short distance to the terminal.

While I waited, I called him on his cellphone. There was no answer. I called a friend in Port Townsend and talked to her for a while, trying to calm myself, attempting to reassure myself.

The tiny plane was full to capacity. With no room in the compartment, my suitcase was stowed in the baggage area. I buckled up, tense and mystified.

The plane taxied to the runway on its trip from Bakersfield to San Francisco airport. As it took off, I felt a sharp jerk as though my connection to Clooney was yanked painfully out of my chest. Trying to remain composed in the tight quarters, I held myself tautly. For ten minutes I tried not to cry.

Then suddenly I sensed a loving unearthly presence. Heard a gentle voice. "I'm here," it said. "I'm always with you." And I relaxed, at peace.

Inexplicably, the same incident happened on the takeoff from San Francisco to Seattle. A sharp pull from my chest. Deep sadness. Then hearing the same voice. Sensing the peaceful presence. I was soothed once again and fell into a deep meditative state, listening to the steady drone of the engines.

I didn't arrive at Seattle until 1:30 AM. The airport was mostly deserted as I made my way to the shuttle pickup. While I waited in the huge underground parking garage, a group of young men hovered a short distance away, voices echoing. Who were they? What were they doing at that hour?

I became afraid. An outcast in an island of cement and garish fluorescent lights. Isolated. Alone in a very big world in the middle of the night. Yet I sensed the calm, loving presence unmistakably with me. Maybe I was capable of making my way safely after all.

I left Clooney a short message. "At Seatac, waiting for shuttle to hotel. Missing you. xxxx"

Eventually the airport hotel shuttle arrived, I was the only passenger. Although shaking with fatigue, I registered, quickly showered, and fell into bed. Only then did I experience sorrow, emptiness, as well as bewilderment. Were we still in a relationship? What was he feeling towards me? Would we still move in together? I had no answers.

As I ate breakfast at a nearby Denny's a sense of loneliness engulfed me again. I had lived with Saul for most of twenty-three years. We were practically inseparable, except for the affair with Clooney. Being adrift in a strange city, with strangers all around, felt spooky and unnatural.

I returned to the hotel in time to catch the shuttle home. I was taciturn and didn't chat with anyone on the return. Anxiety and uncertainty swirled. I left a voice message for Clooney.

A little after noon I was dropped off at my house.

He had left the hotel in Bakersfield soon after I did, not wanting to spend another night in our room, then returned home to work on his taxes.

I was relieved to get his next text.

"Missing you too. Up to my ears with taxes. Sounds like a long night getting to Seatac. xxxxx "

Kisses. From him.

Chapter Twenty One

We talked most every day after my return from Bakersfield, sometimes for hours. I happily anticipated being together and living together. We started planning.

I looked up Clooney's astro-cartography chart to see how Port Townsend would affect him. The chart showed that he would have a dreadful time, maybe even get seriously sick, perhaps die.

"I don't think you should move to Port Townsend," I advised him.

He was undismayed. "Then let's go to Santa Fe, New Mexico instead. I used to live in Albuquerque and love the whole state. I've visited Santa Fe a number of times and always wanted to live there."

I did an astro-cartography chart for each of us. Santa Fe was extremely powerful for both of us. For myself, I had a Venus line running through the area, one of the most auspicious planetary lines in the world to live within. It meant creativity, friendship, relationships, and romance. I had heard that in Santa Fe women outnumbered men 8 to 1. Fortunately I was bringing my lover with me, so that wouldn't be a problem.

"I'll have to lease my house," I announced. "I don't want to put all my belongings in storage, because they are old and it's too expensive. So I'll sell everything."

We discussed dates. A momentous planetary alignment called a Grand Cross was coming up on April 22.

"Let's move in together before the Grand Cross hits," I encouraged him. "How about April 20th?"

"Okay, that's a good day to shoot for," he readily agreed.

I immediately found the best property management firm in town. Within a few days they had signed up an excellent tenant who loved my little house and yard, who had a record of financial stability as well as taking care of the properties they rented.

Clooney and I began sorting through our possessions at our separate homes. I did a practice packing of three suitcases to see what I could fit and what I would need to dispose of. I put ads in the local paper and began selling possessions and furniture. I gave away my beloved king size bed to an elderly couple who didn't have a bed.

As I went along in the sorting, selling, and giving away process, I realized that I would be reducing and eliminating what I owned from many years, including photographs, jewelry, and clothing into the three suitcases.

I went through bins of photos I had carted around through many homes, examining and experiencing each one. Some I sent to my sister and other family members. A few that were left of Saul I mailed to his family. A large box of post cards I had saved from international trips to Europe, England, Scotland, and Egypt, I sent to my grandson. I saved a few dozen photos for myself and the rest I threw in the trash. My past was being eliminated and cleansed. Typical of the Pluto conjunct sun transit that was occurring in my astrological chart.

I wasn't upset. I had moved a lot in my life, each time I mercilessly went through whatever I wasn't using and sold or gave it away. My load continued to get lighter through the years. I also have Uranus in the 8th house of my birth chart, described as: " Your life is characterized by sudden disruptions and events which change the direction of your life quite unexpectedly." So I was used to moving and changing my life numerous times. I had come to be aware that stuff owned me, rather than the other way around. I wasn't very possessive or sentimental. Mostly they were just things. Easily replaced or superfluous.

I gave away the rest of my unsold belongings to Habitat for Humanity. They were grateful to receive the largesse. I gave away my old vehicle, too.

I know from experience, something I call the universal bank account, that whatever I give away comes back to me as I need it, in the form I need it.

At the end of that month Clooney had to travel north to see his accountant to have his taxes done. During those days he called me at night from his motel and we talked and crooned to each other.

He put his house and his two horses up for sale. He went through dozens of boxes of papers, momentos, photographs, and, like me, was throwing most of his earlier life away. He had a huge library of books to go through. The rest of his possessions he was putting in a storage unit, waiting for April 20th.

Clooney told me that Valerie went to work every day and kept herself busy and occupied. They barely talked, the pattern of their relationship for as long as I knew both of them. I wondered if she actually believed he would leave her. Would Clooney finally leave her to be with me? Our past had been complicated and the future was equally vague. I decided not to think about our destiny but to let it reveal itself.

I could hardly believe we were really going to come together, to live together. Holding my breath, counting the days, agonizing and missing him with all my being. Each day harder than the last. Each moment bringing us closer to fruition. My dreams were so near I could smell them.

One night as we talked late he told me, "I adore you."

No one had ever said that to me before. And especially, Clooney had never said that to me before.

Coming from him the meaning was so heartfelt, that it moved me deeply. Was it really him saying those things to me? This man who seldom said what he felt, and kept his deep emotions close to his chest. Did he mean that?

Every day I anxiously waited to hear that he had changed his mind. That we weren't' going to be together. But no. Those words never came. I worried up to the moment when I was getting on the airplane, to fly south with my three suitcases. The plan was for him to pick me up at the smaller airport near Glendale. I wondered. And prayed. And hoped.

My friends had celebrated with me and for me, although some of them worried about my giving away my belongings and moving far away.

I told them, "I have to go. Even if we're only together twenty minutes, I have to do this. I'd regret not going for the rest of my life. I'd wonder if I had made the right decision. For me, there's only this one option."

Despite worries and fear, I kept receiving divine messages that I needed to stay in relationship with Clooney. That our coming together involved healing on a major level. Even though he was old and sick, I needed to be with him. That I was going to Santa Fe, not only to be with him, but because the move involved something bigger for me personally.

I surrendered to those messages. I knew that I could trust my inner messages, even when they didn't make any sense to my logical mind.

Finally the morning of April 20th dawned, sunny and warm, unusual for that time of year in the Pacific Northwest. My waiting had coming to an end. The weather beckoned me. Tulips were blooming. The air smelled of lilacs.

This time there were no delays. I got on the plane on time, heading south to meet my beloved. When I arrived the baggage claim was fast and simple. I put the three suitcases on a wheeled cart and rolled outside into the brilliant sunshine. It was the second time in ten years that I had returned to California. The first was during our short honeymoon in Bakersfield. Hardly the romance capital of the world. Yet it had been for me. Romantic beyond anything I could have ever dared believe.

I called him on my cellphone from the curbside. "Hi, honey. I'm here."

"I'm just entering the airport." He sounded exhausted. He had been sorting and packing for weeks. I saw his truck round a curve.

"I see you sweetheart. I'm over here, to your right." I waved wildly and jumped up and down.

"You're wearing your pink scarf. I see you!" and he stopped in the middle of the lane, as space was jammed at the airport pickup area.

I wheeled each of my suitcases quickly into his truck, not wanting to hold up traffic and stowed them in the back seat.

I jumped in next to him—the place where he had imagined me sitting during his long hero's journey to Port Townsend last December. When I had talked to him nonstop on our cellphones for hours during his trek. He said he could feel me next to him on the wide bench seat all through that dark night.

Now I was with him in the flesh. We could begin our life together. For whatever time that life would allot us. I hugged him tightly, nearly squeezing the breath out of him.

"Not now, honey," he admonished me. "Let's get out of the airport first."

"Okay," I agreed reluctantly, let go of him, and sat back, strapping myself in with the seat belt.

I have clear, quite accurate instincts. Usually I get a tightness in my solar plexus when I intuit something is wrong. I felt that tightness as I sat there, while he maneuvered out of the tiny airport.

Chapter Twenty Two

TENSELY, I SAT NEXT to him while he drove through clogged airport traffic. Then onto a deserted side street. Parking, backing up, and maneuvering was problematic as he drove a massive Ford 350 diesel truck while towing a U-haul trailer behind. He had brought many more belongings than I had.

Finally, after much back and forth, he parked to his satisfaction. He slid out of the truck, went to the back seat and re-arranged my suitcases. He had to urinate, too, so he pissed at the side of the parking curb. Then he climbed back up into the driver's seat.

He had a plan for us to stay two nights in a motel about an hour away from the airport. "To rest and regroup," he explained. He adjusted his sunglasses, rear view mirrors, sun visor, pulled his seat belt tight, and off we went. Never once did he hug or kiss me, or express any happiness in seeing me.

Whenever I tried to talk to him, he interrupted me. "I can't talk and drive. I need to concentrate."

"Okay." I placed my hand gently on his thigh, for encouragement, while attempting to stay connected. We drove in estranged silence.

On Port Townsend's streets and highways, traffic moved at a leisurely pace. Therefore, I was appalled to be in congested California highways again. Cars darted in and out of lanes like insane roadrunners. The speed limit was 65 mph, but everyone drove much faster.

Clooney drove slowly because of the weight and balance of the trailer on the back of the truck. Every time I started to speak, he shushed me. "Not now," he explained tersely.

After waiting to be with him, in my excitement and delight, as well as trepidation towards my epic move to a strange city and state, I found it painful to keep quiet. Like a small excited child harnessed to an edgy, imperious, grumpy parent.

I knew the sensation intimately, having grown up with parents like that. Silence was not only golden, but demanded and reinforced. The tightness in my solar plexus intensified, eventually turning to nausea.

That day, April 20th, was Easter Sunday, but without any Easter celebration. I had hoped for a resurrection of our relationship, but all I got was a dusty tomb. Sitting grim faced next to him, I felt like a sad little girl.

By the time we got to the motel, I was hungry, tired, mildly pissed off, but eager for closeness. We brought in only what we needed and left the rest in his truck.

I undressed and hopped into bed, waiting for him. Wearily he followed suit and laid down next to me. Within a few minutes he was sound asleep. From the experience in Bakersfield, I knew he'd be passed out for hours. This wasn't the life I thought I had signed up for.

Muttering to myself between clenched teeth, I pulled my clothes on, took the room key, my purse, left a note for him, and closed the door behind me.

Not knowing anything about the area, I started walking, figuring a restaurant would be close by the motel, but not the way I went. Feeling highly vulnerable, I turned the other direction and walked a few blocks in the opposite direction, sweating in the southern California heat.

A small Mexican restaurant and bar loomed in the distance. I went in, ordered lemonade, guacamole, and chips. Never comfortable sitting by myself in public eating places, as well as feeling deserted by Clooney, I remained for only ten minutes. Gulping down the rest of the lemonade, I asked the waitress to bring me a takeout box and the check. As if a fugitive from justice, I darted out of the darkened bar and hurried back to the motel. When I returned he turned over and began to awaken, not noticing I had even been gone.

"I have guacamole and chips," I rasped. "Want some?"

"Sure," he replied drowsily.

He reached out and I handed the box to him.

Munching a few, he was quickly satisfied. While he ate, I examined him.

Since the days together in my little apartment/temple, he had withered into an elderly, skinny man of eighty-two with very little appetite. I've noticed that when most men reach their eighties, they seem to lose weight quickly. Sometimes height as well. He used to be 5'11" but now he stood the same height as me—5'7' and stooped.

During the last several years he had lost forty pounds. Although he was still strong, able to wrestle with his Malamute and care for two horses, the flesh on his skeletal arms and legs dangled freely, having lost vital muscle mass.

He'd had gastro-esophageal surgery to correct a hiatal hernia and gastric reflux disease. Instead of ribs naturally tapering down to his abdomen, they came to a squared-off ledge, as though his ribcage was merely a bony mantelpiece. That, plus heart bypass surgery scars from fifteen years before, combined with the weight loss, made his chest misshapen. Rib bones protruded like knitting needles, poking me painfully if I didn't lie against him just right.

He had lost many teeth. Those that were left stuck out at odd angles in his mouth. His slight lisp, helped along by periodically sucking on the stem of a pipe, was more pronounced.

The skin on his hands and forearms was blackened. Was it because of Coumadin, the blood thinner medicine he was taking? Or something else?

His feet and ankles weren't as deeply purple as I remembered them months ago, for which I was thankful. But there were several sores on the bottom of one foot which oozed blood constantly.

"They screwed up on this leg," he pointed to an old, whitish scar running up his calf. "It got badly infected after my heart surgery, the place where my doctor removed the vein to replace in my heart. Almost killed me," he complained angrily.

Since my shocking reaction to him last December, I had diligently practiced visualizing him as the person he had aged into. Not as he used to be—a dynamic man, witty, playful, sensual. Full of energy. Perilously sexy as well, with enormous energy, wearing me out whenever we had made love.

What was I doing with this old man? Leaving everything behind to be with him? He wasn't affectionate. He didn't talk, except to tell protracted tales of his life long ago, of people, places and events unfamiliar to me.

Yet he was the same inside as he'd always been. Only now with physical limitations and changes. Heartbreakingly, I loved him more than ever. I couldn't keep my hands off him. Being around him aroused me as no other man in the world had ever done for me. During the last twenty-five years nothing inside me had changed towards him. I loved him, desired him, even when I didn't want to, or was tired. Any time, even now, when he looked at me with a sidelong glance from his sexy green eyes, I dissolved into a defenseless tangle of passion, love, lust, and connectedness.

He, too, couldn't seem to help himself around me—except now he was worn-out, and had a hard time staying awake.

Nothing could explain our bond that still persisted. We had talked about it endlessly over the phone the last few months, but were stumped for an answer. The only rationale I found—and researched extensively—was we might be twin souls. I emailed him every word I found on the subject.

After that, when leaving messages, Clooney often referred to himself as "your twin." I couldn't positively conclude that we were twin souls. Yet, whatever force operated between us was amazingly powerful, irresistible, and undying over twenty five years.

I had followed him on a life-changing journey, experiencing that timeless connection, believing we could finally be together now.

Yet insecurity entered my thoughts, from the moment he picked me up at the airport. Then watching him, as he was often helpless to stay awake. His moodiness and silent treatment was becoming more unbearable by the day. As if I had returned to my childhood home, shamed into stillness. Invisible. Abandoned. I needed to know if he loved me, but if I asked for confirmation, he'd glower with resentment.

Yet when he was in a sexual mood, he had the ability to draw me unfailingly into bed and into his arms. As corny as it sounds, I practically swooned under his influence, unable to help myself.

When we reached Santa Fe, I worked ceaselessly to find a home for us. I found a lovely furnished condo in a peaceful, gated community and we moved in.

Every day after breakfast he sat on our couch and passed out within moments. Alone, confused, without communication I found myself upset every day. I took walks. Talked to my Port Townsend friends on my cellphone. But nothing helped. The distance between Clooney and me grew. We argued. Misunderstandings erupted over trivial matters.

We were miserable in each other's presence. We even experienced flash backs to our wounded childhoods when together.

What was I to do? I was in a strange town, friendless, alone, without a car, with a mere three suitcases to my name. And only a mute, gloomy, sick, elderly stranger to share space with. I knew our relationship was doomed.

I walked on eggshells around him, unable to know the right thing to say or do. I seemed to upset him easily and often.

One evening during yet another disagreement, he yelled at me. "Our relationship is over!"

"I know," I replied sadly, having come to that conclusion days before.

"Let's be friends at least."

"Okay."

But even being friends didn't work. We still clashed. Had huge differences of opinion. Our unhealed childhoods got in the way of our adult interactions.

Then came the final blow. Clooney stopped having sex with me. I made overtures, but after repeated rejections, I stopped asking. He wouldn't talk about his change of heart except to comment with a statement that wounded me deeply. "You're something. A real horny bitch!"

He wouldn't talk. We slept like two strangers in our bed.

We had been together a mere thirty days, from the airport to the impasse we found ourselves in.

"I'd pack and go somewhere," I told him, "only I have nowhere to go."

"I'll go back to California," he resolved.

Chapter Twenty Three

DURING THOSE LAST DAYS together I grieved deeply. Mourning all the lost years. Forsaken hopes and dreams. Feeling the unful-filled and insatiable desire that still burned in every cell of my body. Knowing that we were not compatible as I thought we were. Only the connection still existed. That connection had kept us coming back over and over for twenty-five years. Now we were leaving each other. It was final. Permanent. Irrevocable.

The night before he left I told him, "I love you, and care for you, and will miss you."

He listened attentively.

I continued. "I don't know if you feel the same way about me. But if you do, could you tell me in words?"

A faint smile of affection played around his lips and crinkled around his eyes. "I love you very much. I care about you. And I'll miss you."

I breathed those words in, letting them sink into my pores.

I watched, with both relief and sadness, as he packed his truck. There was nothing else to do. We couldn't be at peace living together. In fact every day was abject misery for each of us. We rubbed each other the wrong way constantly. With our personalities. Our differences. Our wants. Our needs. Never in my life had I felt so confused and disoriented.

The final morning I walked him out to his truck. Kissed him tenderly on the cheek. He was silent and withdrawn. I watched him drive the truck until he was out of sight.

I would never touch Clooney again. Never kiss him. Never feel his hands on my body. Never yield to his magnetic energy enticing me into passionate abandonment. Never feel the sweet embrace of him. Never hear him moan when we made love. Never to know the magic of our being together.

Never to hear him talk to me with love in his voice. Or to talk to me at all. Or laugh his delightful laugh. Nor hear his endearing names for me, as he told me he adored me.

Never to know his love again.

Never to read words of love or friendship. No words at all. Nothing.

I playacted that he died. That he was unable to communicate with me. That his body was cremated into ash in the heat of a furnace.

But he wasn't dead. He was thoroughly alive. Simply and irrevocably separated from me. Forever. How could I make myself accept forever? I couldn't. I still felt him. As though he was sitting next to me, smiling at me, his delicious lips upturned with subtle humor, teasing me. His warm palm on my cheek. Caressing my fears away.

He still visited me telepathically. I recognized his energy at four in the morning as I awakened to him making love to me. Unmistakable. My body knows his every touch.

A blank piece of paper, starkly white, folded around the apartment key he sent back, spoke volumes, told me plainly he had closed all doors to me. Not even a few words to hang onto.

We hurt each other so much, albeit unintentionally. Our misunderstandings were of gigantic proportions. Our personalities clashed by day as well as night.

Why couldn't we be together? Why were we allowed only mere moments in the vastness of time? Why the long wait…and then another final goodbye? Will I ever know the answers?

One day before he left, he told me, "I can't stay with you—or I'll die."

I understood. I felt the same way.

Yet my emotions and memories tormented me relentlessly. I was overwhelmed with yearning, while at the same time knowing we couldn't be together.

I was mystified at the continued depth of feelings, even after we tried to be together and couldn't, and then separated.

If only I could stop missing him. Stop grieving. Let him go.

I couldn't. I knew I'd love him unceasingly for the rest of my life. The connection remained unbroken.

We had come together many other times in our lives. We had been through so much individually and separately.

Maybe we needed to heal more of ourselves before we could get back together again. Maybe it was about learning, growth, and evolution.

I could still feel him telepathically. He visited me often. I felt his struggles in returning to his wife Valerie and her upset with him.

Our connection is as strong as it always was. Our relationship has only ended for now, on this physical plane, in this moment.

Our bond isn't over. Or I would feel the completion without a doubt. There's more. I know it. Sense it. As though we're connected by a powerful thread, guiding us back to one other. Time after time.

It's our karma.

Chapter Twenty Four

HOW DID I COME to be in my dreadful situation? Desolate in an unfamiliar desert town, four states away from familiar places and faces. Three suitcases to my name. Without a means of transportation to get around. Friendless. Afraid. Bewildered. Adrift and lost.

The man I had loved for twenty-five years had re-entered my life after years of anguish-filled waiting. Passionate longing. Soulful yearning. What joy! His dream, to move to Santa Fe—and with me. I had sold or given away everything I owned. Flew to his side. And he drove us here.

But our coming together wasn't the bliss I believed it would be. Merely personal agony for both of us. After four short weeks he left and returned to his former life. The finality of our decision to split—and my hopes with it—was cruel to confront, but unmistakable. My dream to be reunited with Clooney died, not to be resurrected.

No one was abandoned this time. We left each other by mutual consent. We couldn't live together. Intense pain filled every day simply by being in each other's presence. Nothing ameliorated that agony. Our extreme differences of character, personality, lifestyles, interests, and communication drove us apart. What we needed from each other, to love and feel loved, didn't correspond—although we tried.

"It's like I speak Sanskrit and you speak Swahili," I commented.

"Maybe we're from different planets," he had joked without humor.

So he packed his truck and returned to California. I remained in our tiny furnished condo in Santa Fe, New Mexico, to wait out the duration of the lease we had signed.

I gently kissed him goodbye that final day as he pulled out of the driveway. Then I hid around a corner and watched him drive off, realizing it was the last time I would see him in this or maybe any other lifetime. The sting of his departure hit me hard. All I could do was return to our apartment, lay on my bed, and writhe in agony.

Did he feel grief too? I don't know. He showed little sadness, nor discussed his feelings, that I could know beyond any doubt. Being deeply personal, quiet, and private was his style. He told me he loved me very much and would miss me, but somehow I didn't believe it. Was I grieving by myself? Had I misunderstood him all these years? Or had we changed so much we couldn't tolerate each other?

On the other hand, I had been intensely emotional and talkative, which drove him crazy. Had I pushed him away? All I had were questions without answers.

Part of this perplexing scenario was that for a few days I was relieved he was gone. I felt momentary peace. There was no healing intensity to experience day after grueling day, from waking to sleeping. No more bursting into tears or anger over seemingly-trivial issues.

From the first moment he picked me up at the airport until he returned to California, the anguish for both of us had grown to intolerable proportions. I wept almost every day, except during short intervals when I spent time away from him. I would flee our small apartment as if it was a prison to escape from.

We discussed the mystery of why we felt so terrible with each other. After all these years, why didn't we know? We were dissimilar kinds of people. He withdrew and brooded, or made light of situations. He passed out helplessly for hours almost every day.

I cried and reacted and wanted to talk. When I asked him what he was feeling, he said nothing or made a gesture which meant "don't know." I experienced a shifting vista of emotions, from sadness, grief, confusion to tension, then bouts of anger. As though my body would explode. And several times I did explode verbally, to his annoyance.

The last few days together he didn't make love with me anymore. We used to have boundless sexual appetite for each other during twenty-five years, had experienced wonderful lovemaking often, and could make love for hours on end. So this new desertion was unbearable.

"I miss our intimacy," I told him bluntly.

"I didn't close anything off," he explained. "Just let me know when you want intimacy."

Encouraged I touched him or tried to kiss him, but he pushed me away, with no explanation. Until finally I didn't try anymore.

Lying next to him in bed at night was bewildering as well as agonizing. Do I touch or not touch? Say goodnight or just turn over and go to sleep? Often he thought I was turning away from him when that wasn't my intention at all. Our miscommunication baffled me. When I asked him about it, he seemed wounded that I would mention my confusion, but never explained himself.

Inexplicably, whenever we were around other people, Clooney became playful, chatty, charming, and witty. When he was around someone's dog, he lit up, talked and played with it, petted it. During these times I watched helplessly.

Why didn't he treat me like that? How could I communicate with him? How could I reach him in his world behind a protected shield?

Then within minutes after returning to the privacy of our apartment, he would instantly fall asleep on the couch, often for hours. The inevitability of that gesture never escaped me, although I had no idea what caused him to sleep. Was it illness? Was it the many powerful medications he took that drove him to catatonia? Was it his age? Was it a sleep disorder? Or was he avoiding me?

A few months earlier in the hotel room in Bakersfield, the first time I was faced with his sudden passing out, I tried to talk to him about it. Instead of explaining, he got furious at me, accused me of trying to control him, ready to break up with me there and then.

"I was just sleeping, for god's sake! What is your problem?"

The problem was that his behavior put me at arm's distance from him, all the while I was longing to get close. Intimacy had occurred when we were making love and then disappeared. Now sex was closed off to me too. Not even a subject of discussion.

Then he was gone. He had headed west to California and out of my life.

Twenty-five years of hope, a dream of having a relationship with Clooney, living and playing together, had vanished.

Like the billowy, ephemeral clouds shifting overhead in the turquoise sky of Santa Fe. Then in a moment growing dark and stormy. Wind and rain lashing out at the unprotected ground, creating flash floods within minutes.

"Now what?" I prayed to some unknown higher power, while looking out over the expanse of wind-blown sand and distant naked mountains. "I'm here. You've brought me to this otherworldly town. But for what purpose?"

I heard a soft response. "It's about healing."

I felt an ache in my upper body, a tight knot in my solar plexus.

After Clooney left I was desperate. Scared. Overwhelmed by my situation and my sudden losses. I grieved and started seeing a counselor.

Clooney had desperately wanted to live in Santa Fe. It's ironic that I'm here and he's not. I began to believe that none of our coming together, then separating, was accidental, but purposeful.

I found ACA meetings, adult children of alcoholics and dysfunctional families. I believe ACA is the gift I got from Clooney bringing me to Santa Fe, as there were no meetings near Port Townsend.

I began going to ACA twice a week. I studied the ACA Red Book. Reading it was as though someone had taken dictation of my life's ups and downs, along with my devastating childhood.

I studied with groups and individuals on the Yellow Twelve Steps Study book of ACA, joining the ACA spiritual fellowship and started to find peace.

After a while I realized that the universe, in the guise of Clooney, had brought me here to Santa Fe, this mystical city of vast healing energy, so I could heal my childhood ACA issues. My being here was a miracle, rather than a disaster.

Clooney had been an instrument of the universe. I wouldn't have come here without him. As my loving twin, he had brought me here so I could heal. And then left so I could accomplish recovery on my own, standing on my own two feet. Learning that I could create a new life out of three suitcases and determination – and a spiritual program— including a higher power that can do for me what I could not do for myself.

I've been here almost six months, five of them without Clooney, by myself. I started with three suitcases, no car, no furniture, no household items, a miniscule income, little savings, no home after our four-month lease ran out, and no friends—at first. But that's all changed now.

Our leaving each other created yet another miracle, as Clooney found out about Al-Anon from me. When he returned to California he found local meetings. He now attends four Al-Anon meetings a week. So we're both in a healing process, created as a result of our karmic relationship and deep soul connection, learning to restore ourselves to health and sanity, one day at a time.

During those months, he only answered my phone, text messages, or emails a handful of times. However, he called to inquire of my well-being—as well as to find out how much of the security deposit I was going to send to him.

That inquiry converted something in me. I used to acquiesce to whatever he wanted me to do. Not anymore. I had transformed.

"I'm not going to send you any money from the security deposit," I calmly told Clooney.

"Yes, you are." He disagreed.

"No, I'm not."

"Yes, you are."

"Look, honey. Let's not argue. I'll go over our joint finances again. If I'm wrong, I'll apologize and send you the money. But I don't think I'm mistaken. Because of many costs, I don't owe you anything."

I worked up a statement and found that I was correct. I emailed him a copy.

The day after talking with him and standing up for myself, I felt a shift. An epiphany. Out of the blue I experienced a profound understanding that Clooney now belonged in the past. I was complete with him.

He called in response to my email.

"Hi, sweetie," I answered the phone cheerfully.

I expected Clooney to be furious, but he wasn't. He chuckled at my greeting, then continued peacefully. "I agree with your assessment. We've both spent a lot of money," he said. "So we're even."

"I had a message last night," I continued."

"Oh, what's that?"

"Our relationship belongs in the past. I'm starting a whole new life for myself here in Santa Fe. You are free to do the same. I feel really good about it."

"I think that's called serenity," he answered. He sounded pleased as well as relieved. "I have to go now. Bye bye." He hung up.

Another miracle had transpired. We were released from the centuries-long bondage of hungering, longing, and struggling. I was making a new life for myself without him hovering in the recesses of my mind. The anticipation was gone. Hope and desire had ended and I was free. Free of our everlasting karma.

I bless Clooney for bringing me here. I bless him for leaving. The unraveling of the situation was perfect for the resolution of our long-standing karma. We were lovers no more.

In time I have made dear friends in Santa Fe. I bought a little car and household items, along with some inexpensive furniture. I've fully engaged in a life here. I believe I have been learning to stand on my own two feet. Without him. While detaching from him with love.

I sent him one last text message.

"Thank you for everything, Clooney. I wish you only peace and happiness in your life. Blessings from me. I'll always love you. Your twin."

Glossary

ba: One of the nine souls of the ancient Egyptian religion, it was everything that made an individual unique—similar to the notion of personality

duat: The ancient Egyptian afterlife, supposedly located in the Milky Way, to which souls would return after death

felluca: sailboat on the Nile river in Egypt near Aswan

hemet ntr: ancient Egyptian priestess

hierophant: ancient Egyptian name for high priest

hotep: an ancient Egyptian word that roughly translates to: "be at peace"

khat: one of the nine souls of the ancient Egyptian religion. This was the physical body which would decay after death; the mortal, outward part of the human that could only be preserved by mummification.

khu: one of the nine souls of the ancient Egyptian religion. This was the immortal soul, the radiant and shining being that lived on in the intellect, will, and intentions of the deceased that transfigured death and ascended to the heavens to live with the gods or the imperishable stars.

natron: an important preservative the ancient Egyptians used in their embalming process as well as during sacred rituals. It included sodium chloride (table salt), sodium carbonate, sodium bicarbonate, and sodium sulphate

nemes: the striped headcloth worn by pharaohs in ancient Egypt

Neterw: plural; ancient Egyptian word for god or goddess, meaning energy source

Nuit: An ancient Egyptian Neter (goddess) who lived in the stars and whose body reached over the physical planet Earth, to touch her lover/consort Geb

sesh per ankh hem Sobek: ancient Egyptian male priesthood, including mathematicians, doctors, and scientists, of the crocodile Neter (god) Sobek at the Temple of Kom-Ombo

sistrum: an ancient Egyptian musical instrument, shaped roughly in the form of an ankh, which was played like a rattle

sunu; sunu hemet ntr: ancient Egyptian priestess in charge of health and healing

Was scepter: a symbol that appears often in relics, art, and hieroglyphics associated with the ancient Egyptian religion. It appears as a stylized animal head at the top of a long, straight staff with a forked end.

web hemet ntr: ancient Egyptian priestess who was responsible for the purity of the ritual and the cleanliness of sacred rooms, tools, and paraphenalia.

www.ingramcontent.com/pod-product-compliance
Lightning Source LLC
Chambersburg PA
CBHW071944170626
46813CB00005B/1820